The Lovers

MIKE SA...

Heinemann International Literature and Textbooks
a division of Heinemann Educational Books Ltd
Halley Court, Jordan Hill, Oxford OX2 8EJ

Heinemann: A Division of Reed Publishing (USA) Inc.
361 Hanover Street, Portsmouth, New Hampshire, 03801-3912, USA

Heinemann Educational Books (Nigeria) Ltd
PMB 5205, Ibadan
Heinemann Educational Boleswa
PO Box 10103, Village Post Office, Gaborone, Botswana

LONDON   EDINBURGH   PARIS   MADRID
ATHENS   BOLOGNA   MELBOURNE   SYDNEY
AUCKLAND   SINGAPORE   TOKYO

© Mike Sadler 1993

First published by Heinemann International
Literature and Textbooks
in 1993

The right of Mike Sadler to be identified as the author
of this work has been asserted by him in accordance with the
Copyright, Designs and Patents Act 1988.

British Library Cataloguing in Publication Data
A catalogue record for this book is available from the British Library.

Cover illustration by Max Schindler
Cover and text design by Threefold Design

ISBN 0435 934 309

Phototypeset by
Cambridge Composing (UK) Ltd, Cambridge
Printed and bound in Great Britain
by Cox & Wyman Ltd, Reading, Berkshire

Contents

1	The Rivals	1
2	A Warning	8
3	He's So Cheeky!	11
4	Triumph and Defeat	20
5	Love at Death's Door	29
6	A Misunderstanding	36
7	Long-distance Love	45
8	Show-down	51
9	A Test of Love	59
10	Reunited	69
11	A Promise	79
12	Joy and Pain	85
13	Time for Work!	93
14	Disaster Strikes!	99
15	A New Day Dawns	113

To Eileen

1

The Rivals

As the red sun was setting one hot night in Lapula, an eastern suburb of Johannesburg, the train from the city pulled into the railway station. Passengers spilled out on to the platform.

Sergeant Mogale and Constable Mopani, of the South African Police, sat in their patrol car, watching the passengers arrive. A young woman came out of the station, and stood on the pavement in front of them. She was of medium height, with a long, graceful neck. She had large, dark eyes and a round, pale face.

A fourteen-year-old boy was standing on the pavement, playing a merry tune on a harmonica. Through the large holes in his ragged shirt and trousers one could see his thin black body.

The young woman gave him a twenty-cent piece. 'Go and get yourself something to eat,' she said. The boy smiled broadly, then played and danced again, rocking his head from side to side to show how pleased he was. A large black Mercedes drew up on the opposite side of the road. The driver blew his hooter and waved urgently to the young woman.

'Hurry up, Nomalanga,' he shouted. Then he noticed the police van. He leaned out of the car window, and called out to the sergeant.

Sergeant Mogale walked slowly across the road. 'Good afternoon, Mr Ndlovu,' he said. 'Can I help you?'

'Good afternoon, Sergeant. I have given permission for a group, called the Cats, to give a concert in the social centre tonight,' Mr Ndlovu said. 'But I hear that the Old Block gang are planning to raid the place.'

'Who told you that?' Sergeant Mogale asked.

'Never mind who told me,' Mr Ndlovu replied. 'We don't want another fight between the Old Block and the New Block. Can you arrange to have some extra men on patrol, or must I call up the Police Commandant?'

'No, Mr Ndlovu,' Sergeant Mogale shook his grey head wearily. 'There is usually trouble in Lapula on a Saturday night. I have already arranged for the reserve police to come on duty.'

'Good,' said Mr Ndlovu. 'Then I hope I can spend a quiet evening at home with my family, and not be called out to do your job for you.'

Sergeant Mogale returned to the patrol car. 'You see that man?' he said to Constable Mopani.

'No, no. I was looking at the young woman who got into the car,' Constable Mopani replied, smiling broadly. 'Yoh! Yoh! Yoh! That is a beauty. I could just take her in my arms . . .'

'You had better leave her alone,' Sergeant Mogale interrupted him. 'That is Nomalanga, the daughter of the great Mr Ndlovu. And Mr Ndlovu is the chairman of the council. You will get into big trouble if you try to play about with her.'

'Why do you call him the great Mr Ndlovu?' Constable Mopani asked.

'Do you see the supermarket over there?' Sergeant Mogale replied, pointing across the road. Beyond the car park, Constable Mopani could see a number of shops, joined by a wide tarred street. The biggest shop, BOXERS SUPERMARKETS, was at the end of the street.

'Mr Ndlovu is the manager of the Lapula branch of Boxers,' Sergeant Mogale explained. 'And do you see the big, two-storey building on the opposite side? That is the social centre and the council offices. Mr Ndlovu is also chairman of the Housing Committee and the school board. That is why I call him the great Mr Ndlovu.'

'What did he want?' Constable Mopani asked.

'He told me that the gang from the Old Block are planning to make a raid on the social centre tonight. The Cats are playing there. Lots of people from the New Block will be there, so there's bound to be fighting.'

'Are they always fighting each other?'

'Yes. It's an awkward situation,' the sergeant replied. 'Old Block is old Lapula, where the people first built shanty-houses on an empty piece of ground which nobody was using. Then the authorities decided it was unhealthy. People were getting sick. So they started to build these little two-roomed houses over in New Block. But they did not have enough money to finish the job. Boxers gave them the money to finish the job – provided they could build their shop here and house all their staff. Now Boxers and the great Mr Ndlovu are the managers of Lapula.'

Sergeant Mogale drove away. As they crossed a dry river-bed, he stopped. In front of the two policemen lay a flat, open area of bushveld where people had dumped rubbish, such as old motor cars, broken mattresses, rusty stoves. There was even an old bus.

'This is the dump,' Sergeant Mogale said. 'On Saturday night, three weeks ago, the two gangs had a fight here. Luckily they only used sticks, bicycle chains and knobkerries. Next time somebody will get killed. They are starting to collect knives, spears and daggers.'

'Are they *tsotsi* gangs? Do they steal?' Constable Mopani asked.

'No, they only fight each other,' Sergeant Mogale replied, driving towards Old Block. 'However, one of the boys from the Old Block gang has started stealing cars in New Block. He just goes for a ride and then leaves the car in the dump. The New Block gang have formed a vigilante committee under Cuthbert, Mr Ndlovu's son. They go round the streets at night. If they see any young man from Old Block, they beat him up.'

'Do you know who is stealing the cars?' Constable Mogale asked.

'Yes, we think it is a young man called Makalima, but we can't catch him. He is friends with a young man called Themba who arrived in town about three months ago. We're keeping an eye on both of them.' Sergeant Mogale suddenly jammed on the brakes. 'That's him!' he said. 'Let's see if we can get any information out of him.'

Sergeant Mogale leaned out of the window. 'Hey, Themba Mtuze,' he called out. 'Are the Old Block gang planning to make trouble tonight?'

Themba gave the sergeant a broad grin, showing a set of strong, white teeth and said, 'I am not one of the Old Block gang.'

'Well, tell your friends not to make trouble tonight. I will be watching out for them.'

'All right, I'll tell them if I see them,' Themba promised. 'Now, how about a lift, Sergeant, seeing you are going my way?'

It was a cheeky request, but there was something about Themba that people couldn't resist. Sergeant Mogale laughed. 'OK. Jump in then. This is Constable Mopani.' Sergeant Mogale drove on, past the old beer hall, the trading shops and the dirty marketplace.

Themba was heading for the home of Mr and Mrs Ngxolo where he had been living for the past few months.

The Xhosa word *ngxolo* means 'noise', and it was a good name for the Ngxolo family, for there were seven noisy children. Theirs was one of the better houses in Old Block, made of mud bricks, dried in the sun. There was a living-room with a table and four chairs, and a bedroom which contained the family's proudest possession – an iron double bed. Themba had a separate lean-to room at the back.

'You want some coffee?' Mrs Ngxolo called out from the open fire in the back yard, as she saw Themba coming round to the back of the house.

'Yes, I would like some. But first I must wash,' Themba replied. He picked up the bucket and started walking off to fetch water from the tap.

'I will get the water for you,' Noluvuyo, the eldest daughter, said. She grabbed the bucket out of Themba's hand and started running with it, but Themba caught her by the shoulder and got hold of the handle of the bucket. He pulled and she pulled.

'Why do you want to get the water?' Themba asked, laughing.

'It is not work for a man,' she replied. 'Fetching water is woman's work.'

'Work is work,' Themba replied. 'There is not woman's work and man's work – except for having babies; that is the only work which men cannot do.' He took her hand and pulled it firmly away from the handle. 'But you can come with me, if you like,' he added. 'Then we can talk.'

Noluvuyo looked away from him. She looked down at the ground. She felt shy when this big man stood near her. She was only sixteen years old – still a schoolgirl. But she was not too young to know when a man was handsome, or to love him and wish he would love her. But to be seen walking beside him down Twenty-three Street – that would be too much. Her friends would see them walking together. They would laugh at her and shout rude words at both of them. Themba might get angry. No, no. She could not do that. If only she were older . . .

Her mother saw Noluvuyo's difficulty and called out to her, 'Come here Noluvuyo. Stop worrying Mr Mtuze. Go and get some more wood from the shed.'

Noluvuyo bit her lip with embarrassment, then she muttered, 'Yes, Mama,' and moved away. Themba laughed. 'See you!' he called out and set off down the road.

Five minutes later he strolled into his bedroom with a bucket of water. Themba's bed was made from planks laid across boxes, with two sacks filled with straw for a mattress. He had a small table and chair, a cupboard in the corner and a guitar hanging on a nail on the wall. From under his bed, he pulled out a zinc basin which he filled with water.

He was a tall, well-built man, with long, muscular arms and legs. His broad shoulders and deep chest were covered with fine brick dust from the building site where he worked. His black skin gleamed in the light from the window. While he was putting on a clean pair of jeans and a red T-shirt there was a loud knock at the door.

'It's me, Makalima,' said a voice.

Standing on the doorstep was a small, slight man, his hands clasped together in front of him. He pulled his fingers nervously, so that they clicked. 'Do you want to come with me tonight?' he asked.

'It depends what you are going to do,' Themba said. 'I saw Sergeant Mogale this afternoon. He told me to tell you not to make trouble at the social centre tonight. He will be watching out for you. Is that where you are going?'

Makalima sat on the bed. 'No,' he said. 'But I wish you'd join us. You live here in Old Block, and you see how those smart dickies live over there in New Block. We could give them a good beating. You can be our chief.'

Themba shook his head. 'No thank you, Makalima,' he said. 'I'm not interested in fighting. And if you did give them a good beating, it would make things worse.'

Makalima walked over to Themba's guitar. He ran his fingers across the strings. 'I plan some sport for tonight,' he said. 'There's a smart looking BMW in Forty-seven Street. I've got a key to fit it. I thought I would like to do a zoom. Do you want to come?'

Themba shook his head. 'No thank you,' he said. 'I have other plans. Why do you steal other people's cars?'

'I don't steal them. I only borrow them for the night,' Makalima replied. 'I know that I will never be able to buy a fast car for myself. So, I borrow a car, drive it as fast as it can go, just for the thrill. So I am happy. Then I return it to the dump, undamaged. So the owner is happy. And the police don't have to look for the stolen car, so they are happy. Everyone's happy. What's wrong with that?'

Themba laughed and shook his head. 'Well I am going to the Cats' concert. Be careful. The New Block gang are watching out for you.'

'Don't worry about me,' Makalima said, getting up off the bed. 'I know how to look after myself, see?' He brought his hand out of his pocket. There was a flash of light reflected from a window. Makalima stood holding a knife with a twelve-centimetre blade in his hand.

Themba leaned over and casually lifted Makalima off the ground. Then he shook him – as a dog shakes a rat. 'Drop that knife,' he growled. 'A knife can get you into big trouble!' Makalima dropped the knife and Themba set him back on his feet again.

'Thank you, grandfather,' Makalima said, picking up his knife. 'Chah, friend! Have a happy time with Cuthbert at the concert.'

2

A Warning

'I am not sure if I can trust Sergeant Mogale,' Mr Ndlovu said to his wife, as they drove away from the sergeant's van in their big Mercedes. 'Sometimes I think he is on the side of the Old Block gang.'

'Then you should speak to the Police Commandant. He could move him to another location,' Mrs Ndlovu replied.

'Perhaps I'll do that,' he agreed.

They drove through New Block to a small hill called Imitikop, overlooking the town. The houses here were all large. They were for the managers of the shops, the officials in the township offices, the important people of Lapula. The Mercedes turned into the driveway of the largest of the houses – the one reserved for the Manager of Boxers Supermarket. As Mr and Mrs Ndlovu and Nomalanga got out of the car, the front door of the house was opened for them by a maid in a white apron.

'Bring tea in the lounge, Annie,' Mrs Ndlovu said, as they went through the door into the passageway.

'I won't have tea, Mama,' Nomalanga said. 'I think I'll go and have a shower and lie down.'

'What's wrong with you, Nomalanga? Are you feeling ill?'

'I don't know.' Nomalanga's pretty face clouded over with a frown. 'I think everything is too easy for us. Sometimes I wish we were like those people in Old Block. They may have to struggle to live, but they are much happier than we are . . . They work and save . . .'

'Don't be silly!' Mrs Ndlovu interrupted her. 'You don't know what you are talking about. It is not nice being poor. You are very lucky. Your father has a good job. We have enough money, a big house, a good car. You should thank

God for those things – not waste your time wishing that you were poor. Now, go and lie down on your bed and have a rest. Then come and watch tv with us in the lounge while Annie gets the supper ready.'

Half an hour later there was a knock at Nomalanga's door.

'It is me, Cuthbert. I want to tell you something.'

She opened the door. 'What's the problem?'

'No problem,' Cuthbert said. 'I just wanted to warn you not to go to the concert tonight. There could be trouble.'

Cuthbert was a tall, slender young man of twenty-three. He was one of the up-and-coming young men of Lapula. He held his head high and had a smile on his clever face. It was the sort of smile that seemed to say, 'I know where I am going – and don't try to stop me.'

'How do you know there's going to be trouble?' Nomalanga asked.

'A little mouse told me,' Cuthbert answered, grinning. 'We think the Old Block gang are going to make trouble.'

'No, you don't think that,' Nomalanga replied. 'You and the rest of your gang want to stop them from going to the concert. You are the ones who are going to make trouble. That's the truth, isn't it?'

'Well, why should they come and take up all the seats? This is our centre, our hall, where we have our concerts. If they want a hall, they must build one themselves. That is what we think. So we are going to stand outside the door and stop them from going into the hall.'

'Cuthbert, that is not right,' Nomalanga said. 'The social centre was built for all the people in Lapula – not just the ones living in New Block. You should not try to stop the Old Block people from coming to the concert. Some of them are very nice people,' Nomalanga added. 'I meet them every day in the council office. There is nothing wrong with them.'

'They are poor,' Cuthbert said. 'They do not wash their bodies. They smell. They dress in old clothes. Hah! I don't let them come into the men's department at Boxer's. They do not come there to buy things. They come to look, to feel, to touch and to steal. I'm not stupid. I know what they want.'

'I am going to the concert tonight, Cuthbert. I want to hear the Cats. It is not often that we get one of the top *kwela* groups playing here in Lapula. Also, there is a talent competition. In fact,' she paused for a moment, 'I want to sing and play in the competition.' As she said this, she smiled and her eyes lit up. 'It is going to be great – exciting – you'll see.' Nomalanga closed the door.

'I'll give you a lift on my Yamaha,' Cuthbert called out to her. 'And if there is trouble, look out for me. I will come and rescue you.'

Nomalanga started looking in her drawers for clothes. She found a light-blue mini-skirt and a red T-shirt, which she thought would be just right for the concert.

After she had dressed, she took out her harmonica from its case. She polished it with a soft cloth and blew the notes to warm it up. Then she played the latest *kwela* hit tune, 'Hullo there, Sunshine.' It was, of course, quite a simple tune, but Nomalanga put in some clever little runs which made it sound extra special. Then she sang the words. First she sang in a lovely, clear, high soprano voice. Then she sang in a deep, husky voice. She decided this was the right sound for this kind of music.

When she'd finished, she checked herself in the mirror. She decided to wear a blue scarf around her neck. It matched nicely with her blue mini-skirt, and contrasted well with the red T-shirt.

After supper she announced that she was going to the social centre to attend the concert. At first her parents refused to let her go, but when Cuthbert said that he would take her, and bring her back if there was any trouble, they agreed.

3

He's So Cheeky!

Themba arrived at the social centre with his guitar tied across his back. There was an excited crowd standing outside the entrance doors, waiting to go in. He joined them and started talking to a young man named Pitso, who said he lived in New Block. A bus arrived with more people and a little while later, a big, maroon-coloured motor bike came roaring up to the centre with two people in leather jackets and crash helmets. The driver waved to a group of young men standing at the door and then drove round to the back of the social centre.

'You see that?' Pitso said to Themba. 'That was Cuthbert Ndlovu, and his sister. He's gone to park his motor bike in the back yard. If he didn't do that, the Old Block gang would smash it up. They are a bad lot. Those men in the front are watching out for them. They are Cuthbert's friends.'

Themba noticed the young men standing by the door with sticks in their hands. It was true then, he thought, the New Block gang had come to make trouble. A moment later, a lorry came down Mandela Road and stopped outside the entrance. It was loaded with a dozen policemen, who got down one by one and lined up beside the lorry. The atmosphere was tense and the crowd moved away from the police nervously. A few people started shouting insults at them, but they took no notice and marched forward into the crowd. When they got to where the men with sticks were standing, Sergeant Mogale stopped.

'And why have you brought sticks to a concert?' he asked. 'Can you play music on sticks? Or have you come to beat up the Cats?'

'The Old Block gang are coming to make trouble at the concert,' one of the men said.

'If the Old Block gang make trouble, then that, my friend, is our job,' Sergeant Mogale said. 'We are here to stop trouble-makers from spoiling the concert – wherever they're from. Now, either you give us your sticks, or you leave. Which will it be?'

Two of the men with sticks moved off, muttering to each other. The other two surrendered their sticks to the police, while the crowd stood around and jeered at them. A minute later the glass front doors were opened and the crowd surged into the entrance-hall.

In the lobby of the social centre hall, there were two booking-office windows. The police pushed the people into two queues. On the left side of the lobby were stairs leading up to the council offices on the first floor. A man wearing a black costume, with red and silver trimmings was sitting by the stairs. In large white letters on the front of his costume was the word 'CATS', and beneath it was the picture of a cat with an arched back and a raised tail sewn in silver thread. On the table, in front of the man, was a printed poster.

TALENT COMPETITION
* * *
THIS IS YOUR CHANCE TO BECOME FAMOUS
You too could become as famous as the
CATS
Take part in our Talent Competition
All Competitors will be awarded prizes
THE WINNER WILL BE ABLE TO PERFORM WITH US
AT OUR NEXT S.A.B.C. RECORDED CONCERT IN SOWETO

Themba bought his ticket and went across to the table to enter for the talent competition. The man had a thin, worried face. He peered at Themba and then passed him a sheet of paper and asked him to fill it in. Themba wrote:

NAME: *Mr Themba Mtuze*
ADDRESS: *69, Twenty-three Street, Old Block, Lapula*
AGE: *26*
TYPE OF ITEM: *Guitar and song*
TITLE OF MUSIC: *Hullo there, Sunshine*

The man looked even more worried.

'Can you sing another song – a different one?' he asked.

'Why?' Themba asked. 'What is wrong with this one?'

'There is nothing wrong with it,' the man replied anxiously. 'But see, my friend, it is just that there is another person who also wants to sing that song. It will be better if you sing something else. People will not want to hear the same song twice.'

'No,' Themba said. 'That is the song I have been practising. The other person can sing another song. Or we will both sing it.'

'Hey! That's a very good idea. This person plays a harmonica and sings. You play a guitar and sing. That would make a super duo. What about it?'

'No,' Themba replied. 'I would rather sing on my own.'

'Well, take this upstairs to Simon – that is, Mr Pilane,' the man said, handing Themba his form back. 'He is arranging the talent competition. You will find him in the council room.'

Themba went up the stairs. At the far end of the council room were a very tall thin man and a very short woman standing side by side. They too were dressed in black, red and silver costumes. About ten other people were standing talking to them. Nobody took any notice of Themba.

'Excuse me,' Themba called out. 'Is Simon Pilane here?'

'Here I am,' the tall, thin man replied.

Themba went over to where Mr Pilane and the others

were standing. 'I'm sorry,' he said. 'But there is a problem. I understand that somebody else wants to sing the same song that I have chosen.'

'Oh yes,' the man replied, looking at Themba's form. 'You want to sing "Hullo there, Sunshine". And so do you, don't you Nomalanga?' He turned to a young woman dressed in a light-blue mini-skirt, with a red T-shirt, and a blue scarf. She turned to look at Themba and, as she did so, it seemed to him that time stood still. She had the prettiest face he had ever seen. He stood there like a dumb man, wanting to greet this beautiful young woman, but no sound would come out of his mouth.

'She got here first, you know,' Simon said. 'What do you think, Nomalanga? What do you want to do about it?'

Nomalanga was annoyed that someone else should have chosen her song. But, when she turned to look at Themba, she could not help smiling at him. And he smiled back, revealing a great, wide, white flash of teeth. She turned away, embarrassed by his response. Trying to hide her feelings, she said as coldly as she could, 'Can we go somewhere and discuss this?'

'With pleasure,' Themba replied and beamed again.

'Go ahead,' Simon called after them. 'Perhaps you could sing it as a duo?'

Suddenly, this seemed to Themba to be a very reasonable suggestion. He couldn't think of anything nicer than being with this beautiful young woman for the evening.

'Yes,' he said. 'That's an excellent idea. Don't you think so, Sweetheart?'

Nomalanga stiffened and threw an angry glance at him. 'Who does he think he is?' she asked herself. 'He's got a real cheek calling me "Sweetheart". I bet he thinks he can smooth talk any woman,' she thought.

'I don't think it is suitable as a duo,' she said, in reply to his question. But as she said this she found herself admiring this tall, strong, handsome man. She was immediately furious with herself for admiring his physique. 'I bet he's more suited to wrestling or playing rugby than singing and playing a guitar,' she told herself firmly.

'Hey man, they look real cute together!' the small Cat woman said, in an American accent. She pointed at them and laughed. 'See? They're both in blue and red. They look like they belong. I like it. I like it.'

'Yeah, it's great,' the tall thin man said. 'Go and find a place to practise. You'll need to have a quick run-through. Come back in twenty minutes.'

'Come, Themba,' Nomalanga said. 'I work for the council. Let's go to my office.' She took a key from her handbag and opened the door into the general office. She was sure that one quick run-through would prove that they were not suited to each other.

'Let's talk,' he said, smiling invitingly.

Nomalanga noticed how firm and strong his chin looked. But she had no wish for the kind of talking that he seemed to expect. She pulled her harmonica out of her handbag and blew a few notes on it.

'I am sorry,' she said, as though she suffered from some disease. 'I play the harmonica.'

'That's good,' Themba said. 'I would like to hear you play.'

'First we must make sure we are in tune,' Nomalanga said in a business-like way.

'Yes, of course,' Themba replied. 'Can you give me an E?'

Nomalanga played an E on her harmonica and Themba skilfully adjusted the top string of his guitar until the two notes sounded the same. While he adjusted the other strings, he looked carefully at Nomalanga. Her neck arched gracefully as she bent her head. Her eyes were like two deep pools of water, but when she frowned, it was as though a cloud came over the sun. She certainly was the most beautiful woman he'd ever seen.

'Let's play one verse and one chorus. OK?' Nomalanga suggested.

She played the tune on her harmonica, while Themba accompanied her on his guitar. She expected he would play the guitarist's usual repetitive strumming. Instead, he played with a sensitivity which surprised her. He was not only a good guitarist. He was also an excellent accompanist. Nomalanga began to enjoy herself.

'That sounded OK,' Themba said, looking at her legs. The mini-skirt showed up the lovely slim shape of her thighs and calves. 'What did you think?' he asked, leaning his guitar against the chair.

'You are a good guitar-player,' Nomalanga replied, carefully. She didn't want to admit to him how impressed she was with his playing.

'I'd like to hear you sing,' Themba said. 'I sing bass.'

'I suggest I play my harmonica and sing the first verse,' Nomalanga said. She was surprised to hear herself saying this. 'Why am I suddenly agreeing to this duo idea?' she thought.

She turned to Themba and said, 'I think, you should sing the second verse and we both sing the middle part and the last verse together. How does that seem to you?'

'OK, lady,' Themba agreed, grinning.

They went through the routine, just as she had suggested and, except for one or two minor alterations, it seemed to suit them both.

As they went downstairs to the hall, Themba put his arm comfortably around Nomalanga's slim waist, but she thumped him in the chest with her elbow. 'Don't do that,' she hissed at him. He just grinned his big, wide, white-toothed grin at her. Nomalanga felt angry with him but, at the same time, he was very handsome – and a wonderful guitarist. What more could she ask? 'We'll make these Cats look like miserable frogs,' she thought to herself.

———— ♥ ————

While Nomalanga and Themba were practising, Cuthbert was already sitting in his seat near the back of the hall. Suddenly, Vusi and Takalani, two other members of the New Block gang, appeared. They were supposed to be guarding the front entrance, to keep the Old Block gang away.

'What are you doing here?' Cuthbert demanded. 'Where are your sticks?'

They explained to Cuthbert what had happened. 'And anyway,' Vusi said, as he ended his story, 'we didn't see any of the Old Block gang in the crowd. Perhaps they won't come to the concert.'

'Hah!' said Cuthbert scornfully. 'We will still keep our eyes open. I just hope one of them comes in. I'll tell him smartly we don't want him in here. We don't have to have sticks to beat those boys from the Old Block. I know how to do karate fighting.'

Other followers and friends arrived and soon they were busy talking about the Cats and the songs they liked best. In fact, they were so busy talking that they did not notice when Nomalanga and Themba were taken through the hall by one of the band. All the competitors were taken right to the front row, where seats had been reserved for them.

Suddenly, the lights were dimmed, the curtains drawn aside, and there were the Cats. They were all dressed in the same silver, red and black costumes, which gleamed in the coloured lights. They started playing and singing, and soon the smoke, the noise and all the excitement of a *kwela* concert was in full swing. The war between the Old Block gang and the New Block gang was forgotten in the beat of the drums, the loud songs and the shrill crying of the guitars.

There were six Cats. Two were at the back of the stage.

There was a short, angry man with a thick neck and a broad, flat head. He played the drums as though he hated them. His arms flailed around like a windmill, from chattering drum to clanging cymbal. The other was the tall, thin man who stood behind an electric keyboard. He played with a faraway look on his face, as if he were dreaming.

The other four Cats stood in a line in the front of the stage, behind four microphones. In the centre was Madala, the lead player. He was the old man of the group, the one with the worried face. Next to him was the small woman with the big American voice. She was the main vocalist.

The four front-line players swayed their bodies in time to the music. But it was the small vocalist who caught everyone's eye. Her sinewy body, with the shiny red stripes on the sides of her black costume, swayed back and forth and side to side, like seaweed in water. She had painted large yellow patches around her eyes, which made them look larger. As she rolled her eyes from side to side, the audience swayed with her. Her voice came over the loud-speakers in a hoarse whisper, telling secrets of the heart. Everyone in the audience sat on the edges of the chairs, sang, swayed, stamped their feet and sighed with pleasure. There was no doubt about it, the Cats were hot stuff!

After an hour, Madala announced that they were going to have a break for thirty minutes. The lights were turned up and everyone started moving out to the entrance hall.

Cuthbert reminded Vusi and Takalani to keep a look out for any of the Old Block gang as they joined the crowd. But he was disappointed to find that there were no enemies amongst them.

Once more the lights were dimmed and Madala announced, 'The talent competition is about to begin. There will be four items and you will be the judges.' (A great cheer from the audience.) 'You must try to think which of the items you like best. I will explain what you must do, when they have all finished. OK?' (More shouts and cheers.) Madala held up his hand for silence. 'The first item is a song, "Why did you leave me?", sung by Nosipho. Give her a big hand.'

Everybody clapped as a plump young woman dressed in a bright orange dress came on to the stage. She was followed by a nervous guitarist wearing a pair of large, old-fashioned spectacles. He played a few chords, and the young woman started singing in a loud, very high voice. It was the wrong sort of song for the singer, and the wrong song for such a concert, but the audience kindly clapped, and one or two young men even whistled. Perhaps they were her friends, because she looked in their direction and waved.

This was followed by a young man who played a guitar and sang a song about a lonely mother in a village, waiting for her man to come back from Egoli. By the time he had sung the second verse, the people in the audience had started talking to each other, and long before he reached the end they were shouting for him to stop.

'I don't know why they let him sing,' Takalani said. 'I want to hear the Cats. This competition is a waste of time.'

The next item was a choir of four men and three women, who were actually very good. Well, they would have been good in a church, but a Cats' concert was not the place for them. They sang,

> As we look around the world we can see
> God's goodness lasts till eternity.

And it seemed to the audience that they would go on singing till eternity, but at last they finished.

4

Triumph and Defeat

Then Themba and Nomalanga came on to the stage.

Takalani turned to Cuthbert and said, 'Hey, isn't that your sister with that newcomer from the Old Block? What's she doing with someone like that?'

Cuthbert looked in amazement at the couple. 'She can't know who he is. I'll soon sort him out. I'll teach him to hang about with my sister.'

However, there was no time for Cuthbert to do anything. The audience was becoming restless and people were shouting out for the Cats to return to the stage. Nomalanga looked anxiously at Themba and wondered whether they ought to give up trying to perform. But Themba knew what to do. He advanced to the front of the stage and held up his hand to make an announcement. Soon everyone was silent.

'Good evening, everyone,' Themba said in his deep voice. 'This is Nomalanga. We met for the first time this evening. We found that we both wanted to sing the same tune – "Hullo there, Sunshine".' There was a short burst of applause. Everybody knew this tune. 'So we are going to sing it as a duo. With a one, two, three, four – here we go!'

Themba started playing the introductory chords and Nomalanga stepped up to the microphone. However, instead of singing, as everyone expected, she pulled out her harmonica from behind her back and started playing. There was dead silence in the hall. The audience was impressed. They had not expected anything like this. Nor had they ever heard anything like it before. They sat, as if bewitched by the magic.

When she had played to the end of the first section, she turned and faced Themba, looking up at him as though she adored him. She hoped he wouldn't take this for encouragement since she was merely acting the part which the song required. She sang in her low, husky voice:

> Hullo there, Sunshine,
> D'you want to come with me?
> There's such a lot of things that we could do.
> We could dance and we could sing,
> We could do just anything,
> If only you'd allow me to love you.

People started glancing at each other and smiling, swaying to the music, whispering the words to themselves. They all knew the words. This was good – really good.

When she had finished, she smiled at Themba and waved her hand, as if to say, 'Now it's your turn.' He looked down at her, as though he would like to take her in his arms, and sang in his rich, deep, bass voice:

> Hullo there, Sunshine,
> Why're you holding back?
> Can't you see that I admire you?
> I like the way you walk
> I like the way you talk,
> I like the way you do the things you do.'

Then, while Themba played a twelve-bar introduction, Nomalanga improvised a little dance, by twirling around with her arms held up, and her head on one side. She spun away from Themba, laughing in a teasing way. He was delighted by the way she danced and flirted with him. He didn't realise that she was just play-acting. Nomalanga danced back to Themba, just in time to join him in singing the next verse. But this time she sang the melody in her high, clear, soprano voice, while he sang it in bass. Their voices blended perfectly:

> Isn't it strange
> How alike we are,
> You —
> and me.
> It seems that we
> Both were born
> Under the same old star.

As they finished, Nomalanga raised her harmonica and nodded at Themba. He understood perfectly what she meant and swung into a rhythmic accompaniment. This gave her the chance to put in all the riffs and runs that she could think of.

By now there was a feeling of electric excitement in the hall. There seemed to be a sort of magnetism, which was drawing this young couple together. It was not just that they sang beautifully, and looked beautiful. It seemed that these two singers meant what they were singing. They were in love. This was pure love on display in front of their eyes.

As Nomalanga finished playing, Themba knelt down on one knee to play his guitar, and Nomalanga came and stood behind him, with her arms around his neck. Together they sang the last verse. Themba was overjoyed to have Nomalanga's arms about his neck. He could feel the warmth of her body close to his. Nomalanga realised how happy she was. It felt good to be near Themba.

Now, while she sang the melody, he sang a bass harmony. The sound was rich and warm and sweet:

> Hullo there, Sunshine,
> Just give me your smile,
> And I will take it as your promise true.
> Just give me your hand
> And we'll both understand
> That you love me and I, of course, love you.

As they came to the end of the song, the applause was like thunder. Everyone in the hall rose and clapped and whistled, stamped and shouted, 'MORE! MORE! MORE!'

In the meantime Cuthbert had made his way through the crowd and was walking up the steps on to the stage. 'Come, Nomalanga,' he said.

'What does this man want?' asked Themba.

Cuthbert took no notice. He seized Nomalanga by one arm and started to pull her away. 'Don't you realise this man is one of the Old Block gang,' he shouted.

Nomalanga tried to pull away. 'Let me go,' she cried.

'Leave her alone,' Themba growled, as he swung his guitar by the cord on to his back and grabbed Cuthbert by the shoulders.

This was just what Cuthbert wanted. It gave him a chance to show off his skill at karate. Instead, Themba lifted Cuthbert off the ground, swung him clear of Nomalanga and dropped him on the floor with a crash. Nomalanga was horrified.

Some of the audience thought this was part of the show, and they started clapping, but Cuthbert's friends in the audience were not sure. This was their leader who was being thrown about like a doll. They became angry. Takalani and Vusi rushed up to the stage, shouting 'Get him! Get him!'

Some of the Cats came round from behind the stage curtain and looked on in amazement. The lead player came down stage to stop the fight.

Cuthbert picked himself up. He had not been hurt, of course. One thing he had learned in karate was how to fall on the ground without hurting himself. But he was now very angry. Cuthbert ran towards Themba and leapt up to give him 'a mule-kick' to the head. But Themba had grown up in a rough village in the Ciskei. He knew all sorts of tricks. He was not only big – he was also quick on his feet.

Themba moved to one side, caught one of Cuthbert's feet and tipped him sideways, so that he fell on his back down into the audience. Luckily for Cuthbert, his two faithful friends, Takalani and Vusi, were there to catch him, otherwise he might have been seriously injured.

Themba looked down at them, holding their leader. 'Take him away,' he said. Then he turned to Nomalanga. 'Come, let's go,' he said, smiling calmly. He took Nomalanga's hand before she could say anything, and led her around to the back of the stage – out of sight of the audience.

Madala stepped forward to the microphone. 'QUIET! QUIET EVERYBODY!' he shouted. 'Please get back to your seats.' Some of the New Block gang were trying to climb on to the stage to follow Themba and Nomalanga, but three more of the band rushed from the back and pushed them back into the crowd.

The hall began to look like a battlefield, with men fighting each other in the aisle, and women screaming. Madala kept booming over the loud-speakers, 'QUIET! QUIET!' Suddenly there were a series of shrill whistles from the back of the hall. Everyone stopped to look around. There was Sergeant Mogale with his six policemen, carrying long truncheons, and forcing their way into the hall till at last they reached the stage.

'Are these people giving you trouble?' Sergeant Mogale asked Madala in a loud voice, pointing to Cuthbert and his friends.

'There was some trouble. But it is over now,' Madala replied. 'We want to go on with the concert. Everything is all right now, thank you, Sergeant.'

Sergeant Mogale turned to Cuthbert. 'Your father told me there was going to be trouble at the concert tonight, Mr Cuthbert,' he said. 'He did not tell me that you were going to be the trouble-maker. Now, either you go back quietly to your seat, or I give you a ride to the police station. Which is it going to be?'

Cuthbert turned to his friends. 'Come,' he said to Takalani

and Vusi. They walked out of the hall into the darkness outside.

As Themba and Nomalanga came round to the back of the stage, the woman vocalist threw herself at Nomalanga. 'Are you all right, Honey?' she asked. 'Come! Let's quickly get you out of here.'

Before Nomalanga or Themba could say a word, she and Simon, the long, thin Cat-man, had hustled them out of the back door and into a blue minibus standing nearby. Nomalanga told Simon which way to go. He drove the minibus to Imitikop and stopped outside the Ndlovus' house. The blue minibus swung round in the road and pulled away, leaving Nomalanga and Themba standing in the road.

At last they were alone together. Themba put an arm comfortingly around Nomalanga's waist. She swung round and smacked him across the face.

'Who do you think you are?' she asked. 'Just keep your hands to yourself.'

'But, but . . .' Themba did not know what to say. 'I'm sorry. Is this your home? Then you are the daughter . . .? I did not know . . . I thought . . .'

'Don't bother to explain. I know what you thought,' Nomalanga interrupted. 'You thought that, because I agreed to sing with you, you could put your great, big, dirty paws all over me. Well, you made a mistake. And I'm the one who is sorry. I am sorry I agreed to do it with you. I just hope you did not injure my brother, Cuthbert. If you did, you will be hearing from my father. In any case, I don't ever want to see you again. Is that clear? Never! Never! Never again.'

She turned round and walked away, up the drive to the house. She opened the door and disappeared from view.

Themba stood in the road and watched her go. He could not believe what he had heard her say. It seemed that, only a few minutes ago, she had been looking into his face, and singing in that beautiful voice of hers. And now this – a slap in the face and the message that he was never to see her again. He turned and started stumbling along the dark road back to Old Block.

———— ♥ ————

Mr and Mrs Ndlovu were busy watching television in the lounge when they heard Nomalanga enter the house. 'What is the matter, child?' Mrs Ndlovu asked. She could see something had happened to upset Nomalanga.

'There was trouble at the concert,' Nomalanga replied.

Mr Ndlovu stood up. 'I knew it,' he said. 'Were the police there? I told that sergeant to expect trouble from the Old Block gang.'

'Oh yes,' Nomalanga replied. 'The police were there, but it was Cuthbert and his gang who caused the trouble. They were fighting when I left the hall. I don't know what has happened now.'

'I'd better go and see,' Mr Ndlovu said, standing up. He went out to get an overcoat and a few minutes later, they heard him drive off in the car.

'You had better go to bed,' Mrs Ndlovu said, putting her arm comfortingly around Nomalanga's shoulders. 'Do you want some tea or coffee?' Nomalanga brushed aside her mother's arm.

'I'm all right, Mama. Nothing happened to me. But I don't know what happened to Cuthbert. He may be hurt.'

'Oh, you need not worry about Cuthbert,' said her mother proudly. 'Since he learned karate, I do not worry about him any more.'

'Hah!' Nomalanga replied, shrugging her shoulders. She did not want to tell her mother that Themba had thrown Cuthbert off the stage. When she had last seen Cuthbert, he was being held up by his friends. He was probably quite safe.

Nomalanga poured out a glass of milk and took it to her room. As she sat down on the bed, she felt something in the pocket of her skirt. It was her harmonica. She pulled it out, and suddenly the whole excitement of the evening came flooding back into her mind. She remembered meeting Themba. He really was a very good guitar-player and singer. How the crowd had clapped and cheered. It was a pity that Cuthbert had spoiled it all for them. They would surely have won the competition.

Themba had said, 'What does this man want?' She realised he did not know that Cuthbert was her brother. Nomalanga gasped. 'He must have thought Cuthbert was a jealous lover of mine, coming to beat me up.' She understood now why he had looked so surprised when they stood in the street outside the house. 'Is this your home?' he had said. And he tried to say he was sorry. 'But I slapped his face,' Nomalanga said. Then she threw herself down on the bed, buried her face in the pillow and wept.

Themba trudged on down the road. He decided he would not go back past the social centre. He had no wish to start another fight. As he walked, he too thought back over the events of the evening. It had been wonderful meeting Nomalanga, and playing and singing together. She was the woman he'd dreamed about so many times. He remembered the way her lips curled into a smile, as she sang. He remembered how her steady brown eyes looked up at him. It made his heart beat faster, and he started walking faster in his excitement. Presently he came to Mandela Road and set off towards Old Block.

A few minutes later he heard the sound of a motor bike coming from behind him at high speed. He stepped back into the bushes at the side of the road as it flashed past. A short time later a car, also driving at high speed, passed him. The beam of the lights cut through the darkness ahead and then the tail lights, like two angry eyes, disappeared down the road.

Themba walked on and, as he crossed the dry river-bed, before the dump, he saw a motor bike standing at the side of the road, hidden by some bushes. Just then, he heard a car start up in the road in front of him. It came towards him, and again he stepped aside as it went past. It was the same car that had passed him earlier – going the other way.

A little further on there were some white oil drums standing in the road, with a sign saying, STOP. ROAD UNDER REPAIR. Themba had not noticed them when he walked to the concert earlier in the evening. A short distance beyond this was a footpath which went across the dump. It was a short cut to Five Street. Many people – especially women – were afraid to take this path in the dark. Themba did not worry about this. It saved him ten minutes.

He came to the old, wrecked bus. As Themba walked past it, he heard the sound of a moan, 'Aaaaahhh!' It sounded like someone in pain.

Themba walked over to the passenger's door of the bus and peered inside. He could see the body of a man lying on the floor. There did not seem to be anybody else in the bus. The man was moaning.

Themba climbed into the bus and bent over the man. There was a pale moon shining outside. There was just enough light to see the man's face. It was Makalima – his friend. There was a wound on his head. Blood was coming out of it. 'Hey, Makalima!' Themba said. 'Are you all right? Can you hear me?'

Makalima groaned again. Themba heard a movement behind him. He started to turn around when, suddenly, he felt a sharp pain in his back. He half rose to his feet, but it felt as though somebody was pushing a red-hot iron bar into him. He tried again to face the person – whoever it was – but he felt himself falling . . . falling . . . falling into a great pit of darkness. Then he knew no more.

5

Love at Death's Door

It seemed to Nomalanga that she had just fallen asleep when she heard someone opening the door of her bedroom. She switched on the light next to her bed, and saw Cuthbert standing inside the doorway. His smart clothes were torn and there was blood on his shirt.

Nomalanga sat up in bed and looked at her watch. It was nearly five o'clock in the morning. 'What's the matter, Cuthbert?' she asked. Cuthbert walked slowly across and sat on her bed.

'There is trouble – big trouble,' he said. 'I think the police are looking for me.'

'Why? What have you done?'

'It's the gang from the Old Block . . . that new, big friend of yours, Themba. He is one of them. I did not mean to . . . The police are looking for us. One of them saw me.' He started shivering.

Nomalanga put her hand on Cuthbert's back to comfort him. 'Take it easy,' she said. 'Tell me from the beginning. What happened after I left the hall?'

Cuthbert straightened himself up, and tried to smile at Nomalanga. Then he began his story.

'After you left,' Cuthbert said, 'Sergeant Mogale told us – me and Vusi and Takalani – to leave the hall. Rapula was waiting outside. He said somebody had stolen his car – a second-hand BMW. He phoned the police. They said he must tell Sergeant Mogale at the social centre.'

Nomalanga shivered with the cold and reached for her dressing-gown at the bottom of the bed. Cuthbert continued with his story.

'I told Rapula not to waste time with the police by telling

Sergeant Mogale about it. I had a better way of catching the thief.' Cuthbert smiled. 'You know those white oil drums they put in the road to stop the traffic? Two days ago, I hid some in the bushes in the dump. So, I told Rapula and the other two to take the drums out of the bushes, and roll them along the road to the footpath. Then they were to wait for me in the old bus.'

'What for?' asked Nomalanga.

'So we could catch the thief. I went off on my bike to the old mine dump, near the Jo'burg freeway. From there I could see all the cars going past. When I saw Rapula's car, I took the short cut back to the dump and we pushed the drums into the road. Then we hid away till we heard the car stop behind the drums. Of course, the driver did not know we were there. It was one of the Old Block gang – the small thin one, Makalima. He thought the road was being repaired.'

For a moment, Cuthbert looked pleased with himself. 'That Makalima got a big fright when he saw us coming round from behind the drums,' he said. Then he frowned again, as he remembered the fight. 'Makalima jumped out of the car. He wanted to run away. Rapula caught him by his shirt. Then Makalima pulled out a big knife. But we had our sticks and we beat him up. Yoh! We gave him a good beating. He fell down on the ground and Takalani took away his knife. Then Rapula got into his car. He said he was satisfied and he drove the car away.'

'Then what did you do to Makalima?' Nomalanga asked.

'We dragged him along the path to the old bus. I said we must just leave him there, but the other two beat him up some more. He was only semi-conscious. he just lay on the floor, groaning. Suddenly I heard somebody walking along the path. I was afraid. I went and hid in the bushes. Vusi and Takalani hid in the bus, where the driver sits. The man came closer. It was that man, Themba. I wanted to creep up on him, and beat him with a stick. But Makalima groaned inside the bus. Themba heard him. He stopped and went into the bus and . . . and . . .'

Cuthbert stopped suddenly. He turned his face away from Nomalanga.

'What?' Nomalanga asked. Her voice was high. She wanted to scream. 'What happened?'

'I heard somebody fall down inside the bus, so I ran to see. Themba was lying on top of Makalima. There was a knife in his back. It was Makalima's knife. Blood was coming out very fast from the wound. I pulled him away from Makalima. That is how my shirt got all this blood on it.'

Cuthbert looked down at the blood on his shirt and he shuddered. He remembered again the fear he had felt when he first saw that blood. He had realised then that he and his friends were now in serious trouble.

'I turned around and saw Takalani and Vusi standing in the driver's place. "Who did this?" I asked and Takalani said he did it. I asked him why, and he said that Themba deserved it.'

Cuthbert stopped speaking. He sat looking at nothing, remembering, thinking in fear. He looked up slowly at Nomalanga's face – as if he were asking for help. 'I think . . . I think Themba is dead!' he said.

Nomalanga shuddered. A feeling of numbness came over her. She heard herself asking mechanically, 'What did you do? What happened next?'

'Suddenly we heard the police van coming – the siren got louder and louder as it came near. We were frightened and jumped out of the bus. We could see the police van standing by the drums in the road. Then we started running along the path to Five Street.'

'Did the police see you?'

'Yes, they saw us, but I don't think they knew who we were. They started running after us and shouting. When we got to Five Street, we ran down to the beer hall. There were a lot of men still sitting there drinking, so we sat down amongst them. The police came and looked around but they did not seem to recognise us. After a while they went away, so I went back to my motor bike. I had hidden it in the bushes near to the bus. Then I came home.'

'Do you think the police saw your motor bike?'

'I don't know.'

'If they did, then they will know you were there, where the murder took place.'

'Murder?' Cuthbert asked.

'If Themba is dead, then it is murder, and the police may think you were the one who murdered him,' Nomalanga said. 'Cuthbert, we must go now to the hospital and find out if Themba is alive or not. I want you to take me now, before Mama and Dada are awake.'

'Go to the hospital?' Cuthbert said slowly. He seemed dazed, unable to think of anything.

'Go and wash your hands and face and change your shirt,' Nomalanga said. 'I'll dress quickly and come and join you outside, by your bike. Go quietly.'

Cuthbert nodded and went off. Nomalanga dressed herself in jeans and a blue zip-up jacket and went out quietly through the front door.

Cuthbert was waiting. They pushed the bike out of the gate and down the road. They did not want the noise of the engine to wake Mr and Mrs Ndlovu. When they were far enough away, Cuthbert pressed the starter button and the powerful engine roared into life. They both climbed on and shot away down High Street, heading for the freeway.

Cuthbert drove his motor bike fast along the freeway. It was six o'clock in the morning and there were not many cars on the road. The bike sailed straight down the right-hand lane like an assegai. Cuthbert leaned into the wind, and Nomalanga pressed against his back, holding him around the waist. They turned off at Junction 14, and went along the road to Luthuli Hospital. There, Cuthbert stopped the bike in the car-park, as close as he could to the entrance door. They climbed off the bike and took off their crash-helmets.

'Come!' said Nomalanga briefly. She led the way into the hospital and stopped at the enquiries desk. There was a young nurse behind the counter in her smart pale-blue uniform.

'Can I help you?' she asked Nomalanga.

'Yes, I am looking for a Mr Themba Mtuze. Was he brought into this hospital last night?'

The nurse looked at a large book that was standing on a table behind her. She ran her finger down the page and then stopped. 'Yes,' she said. 'The police brought in a man by that name. It was round about two o'clock this morning. He is in ward 17 K.'

'Is he . . . is he . . . is he still alive then?' Nomalanga asked.

'I don't know. You will have to ask the sister in charge of the ward,' the nurse said. 'It is along that passage, and up the stairs. When you get to the top, turn right and go along till you come to corridor 17. You will find the numbers on the wall. The first door on your right is the sister's office. Ask for Sister Mathebula. She will be able to tell you about Mr Mtuze.'

'Thank you.' Nomalanga soon found herself in the sister's office. Sister Mathebula seemed to be both busy and angry.

'My name is Nomalanga Ndlovu. This is my brother, Cuthbert. I am looking for Mr Themba Mtuze,' Nomalanga explained.

'Are you relatives?'

Nomalanga shook her head.

'Well, you can't see him,' the sister said bluntly. 'He is seriously ill. Nobody can see him. I cannot tell you when he will be able to see visitors. I cannot tell you anything more at present. I am very busy. As I said, he has been very seriously wounded – he was stabbed in the back. The knife went very close to his heart. He lost a lot of blood and he's very weak. We are doing the best we can for him, but he is in a dangerous condition.'

Suddenly Nomalanga felt as though a great wave was going over her. She felt the room spinning around. She felt herself falling. She put her hand on the table to steady herself.

'Watch out!' said Sister Mathebula, catching Nomalanga by the arm. 'What's the matter child? Hey you! Come and help her,' she said to Cuthbert.

Cuthbert held Nomalanga by one arm, while the sister supported her on the other side. Together they led her to a chair and made her sit down. Then Sister Mathebula brought a glass of cold water for her to drink. She leaned over Nomalanga, in a motherly way, supporting her back while Nomalanga sipped at the water.

'Thank you,' she said. 'I'm sorry, I don't know what happened to me. I'm all right now.'

'Are you pregnant?' Sister Mathebula asked bluntly.

At first, Nomalanga felt angry. Who did this sister think she was, asking such a question? It was no business of hers. But her anger made her heart start pumping harder. She started to feel stronger. Then she smiled. Of course, pregnancy and the birth of babies were the business of the sister; it was part of her job. Nomalanga smiled at the motherly face above her.

'Mama!' she said, smiling. 'I am not pregnant. I have not been with any men. But the man I would like for my husband is that man in K ward.' She thought of Themba, slowly dying in a cold room somewhere nearby. There was nobody with him who loved or cared about him.

'Please Sister, let me see him,' she said. 'If he dies, I will always . . .'

'Don't try and tell me you are not pregnant, girl,' Sister

Mathebula replied. 'But if he is the father of your child, then you had better come with me. You can see him for just one minute.'

She led the way along a wide passage. At the end of the passage were two closed doors marked K and L, one on each side of the corridor. A notice on each door said:

QUIET PLEASE! INTENSIVE CARE UNIT.

The sister opened the door of K ward. In the centre of the room was a bed with a patient lying in it. It was difficult to see him because there were so many tubes going into him. A nurse in blue was standing beside the bed, changing one of the bottles attached to one of the tubes. She looked around.

'I have given permission for these visitors to stay just one minute, Nurse. Then they must go,' said the sister.

'Yes, Sister,' the nurse replied.

The sister nodded at Nomalanga, stepped back into the passage and closed the door.

Nomalanga turned slowly and walked towards the foot of the bed. She was afraid to go too close. Yet she desperately wanted to see him again. As she stood at the foot of the bed, she was able to see his face. His eyes were closed, his head hung on one side and his mouth was open. His face was a grey, muddy colour. A plastic tube went into his nose. It looked as though he was already dead, except that his chest heaved slowly up and down. He was still alive. Nomalanga held her breath. She watched his face for signs of life. His mouth started to move . . . he was trying to talk. His eyes opened. At first he looked about without seeming to see anything. Then his eyes focused on Nomalanga. His mouth began to move and then, very softly, Themba spoke.

'Hullo there, Sunshine,' he whispered. He smiled and his eyes closed. His head fell back on the pillow.

'I think you ought to go now,' the nurse said.

Nomalanga stood still and silent, gazing at Themba. Cuthbert put his arm around her waist. 'Come, Nomalanga.'

6

A Misunderstanding

When Themba found himself falling into the pit of darkness, his first thought was that he was going to die. 'I'm going to crash on to the rocks at the bottom of this pit and be killed.' He tried to shout, but no sound came from his throat. Then, like a miracle, he was saved. Instead of rocks, there was a great rushing river of water. He found himself being carried along in a dark passage through caves. At last, he came out into a dark sort of jungle. There were banks on each side of the river, with great trees and creepers.

After a while, he noticed that the water was slowing down. He was now in a huge pool in a cave. The water was slowly swirling round and round. There was a roaring sound coming closer and closer. He raised his head and saw there was a big waterfall. The current was carrying him towards it. Soon he would fall over the edge – to his death!

'I must swim to the side and pull myself out,' Themba thought. So he started trying to swim but the water was very heavy. He could only manage a few strokes. Then he had to rest, but while he was resting, of course, the water carried him nearer to that thundering waterfall. He kept trying to swim, but he felt very weary. At last he thought, 'It is no good. I cannot swim any more. If I go over the waterfall, what does it matter? I am too tired to care.'

He lay back and let himself drift. While he was drifting, he remembered that, just before he fell into this pit, something exciting had happened, something that made him feel happy. He wished that he could remember. 'I'll just try once more to swim to the side,' he thought. So he started swimming again with great, strong strokes. He saw some rocks and seized hold of them. The water dragged at his body, but he held on.

Through a cleft in the rocks, he could see a clump of bushes. There was a clearing, with a shaft of light shining in the centre. There was somebody standing there. The light did not come from above. It came from the person. It was Nomalanga, the woman with the golden voice! He tried to reach out to her.

'Hullo there, Sunshine,' he called out. His voice sounded strange and loud in his ears. He saw her smile at him. Then the water swirled up around him and dragged him away.

Although he was drifting again, he felt quite different now. He did not feel hopeless. He had to keep on swimming for the side of the pool. Soon he would get out of this strong current, on to the land. Then he would find a path to take him back to Nomalanga. He must save her from any wild animals. Nomalanga needed him. He set off swimming steadily for the side. Now he knew what he must do.

———— ♥ ————

When Cuthbert and Nomalanga arrived back at their father's house on the motor bike, they found the police patrol van parked outside the front door. 'Sergeant Mogale wants to see you,' said one of the policemen. Cuthbert nodded. He and Nomalanga went in. Sergeant Mogale was sitting in the lounge with Mr and Mrs Ndlovu.

'Where have you been, Cuthbert?' Mr Ndlovu asked.

'We have been to Luthuli Hospital,' Cuthbert replied.

'We went to see Mr Themba Mtuze,' Nomalanga went on. 'He is a friend of mine.'

'Mtuze is your friend?' Sergeant Mogale was surprised. 'Where did you meet him?' He started writing slowly and carefully in a notebook.

'Themba and I sang together at the Cats' concert last night,' Nomalanga said.

'Last night, Miss Ndlovu, you sang with Themba Mtuze, and you, Mr Cuthbert, fought with the man. Later we saw you running away from the old bus in the dump, and we found your motor bike parked near to it. Inside the bus we found this same Themba Mtuze lying on the floor. Somebody had stabbed him in the back with a knife. This morning, you take your sister to the hospital to visit him.'

The sergeant turned to Mr Ndlovu, 'Does it not seem strange to you, sir?' he asked.

Mr Ndlovu looked at Cuthbert. 'Did you stab Mtuze?'

'No, Dada. I did not stab him,' Cuthbert said. He turned back to Sergeant Mogale. 'We heard people shouting and fighting inside the bus. Some of them ran away. Then we went to look inside the bus and found Mtuze lying there with a knife in his back. I think the people who stabbed him were *dagga*-smokers. Suddenly we heard the police van coming, so we ran away.'

Sergeant Mogale looked over the top of his spectacles at Cuthbert. 'Your friends, Vusi and Takalani were with you. Is that correct?'

'Yes . . . No . . . Yes,' Cuthbert agreed at last.

'You had better come with me,' said Sergeant Mogale. 'Your friends are sitting in the police station now. They have told us a different story. We will have to ask you some more questions.'

'Just a minute,' said Mr Ndlovu. 'If you are going to take my son then I shall phone my lawyer.' There was a phone on the wall in the passage. He spoke briefly into it and returned. 'Mr Gumede is coming immediately,' he said.

'That's all right, Mr Ndlovu,' Sergeant Mogale replied. 'I am not arresting Cuthbert yet,' he said. 'When your lawyer comes, please bring them both to the police station.' He turned to Nomalanga. 'How is your friend, Mr Mtuze?' he asked kindly. 'I hope he has survived the stabbing?'

Nomalanga felt embarrassed. She thought of how he had

whispered, 'Hullo there, Sunshine.' She would never, never forget that.

'He is not dying,' she replied firmly. 'He . . . he is going to live. I think . . . I think he is a good man.' She turned away so that her father and mother could not see the tears that were in her eyes.

'Good.' Sergeant Mogale picked up his helmet and turned to Cuthbert. 'I'll see you at the station,' he said.

As soon as Sergeant Mogale left the room, Mrs Ndlovu started wailing. 'Yahhh!' she cried. 'What have you done? We do not want the police coming into our house. Yahhh! Yahhh! How could you do this to me?'

'Shut up, Dudu,' Mr Ndlovu said to his wife, angrily. He looked at his two children and frowned. 'I am angry with both of you,' he said. 'You have brought disgrace to us. Tell me the truth. Did you stab that Mtuze?'

'No, Dada. It was Takalani who stabbed him. Anyhow, he is only one of the Old Block gang. And it was his friend, Makalima's, fault. He had the knife. It was his knife. He tried to stab us first. So, you see . . .'

'I am not interested in Makalima or Takalani or anyone else,' Mr Ndlovu said. 'I just want Gumede to get you off the charge. Is that clear? You will tell Mr Gumede what really happened – not all those lies you told the sergeant. Mr Gumede will know how we can get you out of this trouble.'

He turned to Nomalanga. 'As for you, my girl,' he said. 'I am going to send you to Ladysmith. You will go and stay with your Aunt Nonzwakazi until you have forgotten about this Mtuze business.'

At that moment, a car pulled into the front yard. A moment later the front-door bell rang. When Mr Ndlovu opened the door, a stout little man, who could have been any age from thirty-five to fifty-five, entered the room. He was going bald, and his bulging eyes stared out seriously at the world. He was not a handsome man, but he was well dressed in a blue suit, and he had a smooth, educated look about him.

Mr Gumede shook hands slowly and seriously with Mr and Mrs Ndlovu, then with Cuthbert and lastly with Nomalanga. But when he took Nomalanga's hand, he held on to it for a moment longer than was necessary. Then he turned to Cuthbert and said, 'I understand that you are in trouble. How can I be of help to you?'

After Mr Gumede was briefed, the men went off together in the Mercedes to the police station.

When they had gone, Mrs Ndlovu turned to Nomalanga. 'I'm sorry, my child, that you have had this trouble,' she said. 'But don't you think Mr Gumede is a fine man? That is the man, Nomalanga, that I would like you to marry. He is kind and clever and rich. You would be very happy if you married him.'

Nomalanga pulled a face. She did not like Mr Gumede.

'As you know Dada has decided that you should go to Aunt Nonzwakazi for a holiday in Ladysmith.'

'But why?' Nomalanga asked. Her eyes flashed with anger. 'I want to stay here and visit Themba in hospital.'

'That is why Dada wants you to go to Ladysmith. He does not approve of your friendship with a man from the Old Block gang,' Mrs Ndlovu said. 'Dada wants to take you by car to Ladysmith this afternoon. You must stay for a month. And you must promise not to write to that man.'

'He is not one of the Old Block gang,' Nomalanga shouted. 'Why do you say he is one of them?'

'Of course he is. Your brother says so,' Mrs Ndlovu answered calmly. 'Anyway, you must start packing your suitcase. I wish I could go and have a holiday with Aunt Nonzwakazi.' Nomalanga reluctantly went to start packing.

When Mr Ndlovu returned with Mr Gumede and Cuthbert from the police station he seemed very pleased.

'Hah!' he said to Mrs Ndlovu, giving her a kiss. 'I can tell you this, Mr Gumede taught that Sergeant Mogale a lesson in law. Mogale thought he could keep Cuthbert in the police station. But you see, when the police saw Cuthbert running away, he was in Five Street. He was nowhere near the bus. That is what Gumede pointed out. I was right to get a good lawyer, wasn't I?'

Mrs Ndlovu threw her arms around Cuthbert, 'My Cuthbert is free!' she said.

'He is not quite free yet,' Mr Gumede said quickly. 'He has to go back to the police station tomorrow for more questioning. But certainly, they are not going to arrest him.'

'I think we should all go to church now,' Mrs Ndlovu said as Nomalanga came back into the room. 'I think we should go and thank God for saving our Cuthbert. We would be very proud to have you sitting with us in church, Mr Gumede – wouldn't we, Nomalanga?' Mrs Ndlovu slipped her hand through Nomalanga's arm.

The church was crowded when they arrived. It was a solid, brick building with high windows and a red carpet. The congregation was already singing. The people always sang hymns while they waited for Reverend Setuki to come. Mr Ndlovu always sat at the end of the front row, because he had to take the collection plate around. Next to him sat Mrs Ndlovu, then Cuthbert (who was her favourite child) and then Nomalanga – the youngest. Mr Gumede sat next to Nomalanga and took her arm. She angrily pushed his hand away, opened her hymn book and started singing.

At last Reverend Setuki arrived and the service began. Reverend Setuki started praying, and Nomalanga started thinking of Themba lying in hospital. She remembered his grey, muddy face. Then suddenly she heard Reverend Setuki say, '. . . and, dear God, we ask you to be with the young man who was brought into Luthuli Hospital with a stab wound during the night. May he know that there are people who love him, and that you love him, O God.'

'Amen! Amen!' shouted an old man at the back of the church.

'Please, please God, don't let Themba die,' Nomalanga prayed. She knew now that she would always love him.

At last the service ended. Reverend Setuki stood at the door, shaking hands with everybody. Mrs Ndlovu proudly introduced Mr Gumede as 'our dear friend'. Mr Gumede quickly stood beside Nomalanga, holding her arm, as though they were lovers.

'Would you two like to come to the Young People's Fellowship meeting this afternoon?' Reverend Setuki asked Mr Gumede and Nomalanga. 'The subject is going to be "Planning for Marriage".'

Mr Gumede said, 'Yes.' Nomalanga said, 'No, thank you.' And Mrs Ndlovu explained that Nomalanga was going away that afternoon to stay with her aunt in Ladysmith.

'Can I come with you, Reverend Setuki?' Mr Gumede asked. 'I would like to offer legal advice to the young people. I am a lawyer.'

'Thank you, Mr Gumede,' Reverend Setuki replied. 'I shall not be there myself. I have to go to visit Lapula patients in the Luthuli Hospital this afternoon. But of course you will be welcome to attend the meeting. I am sure the young people will be glad of your advice.'

The Ndlovu family started moving off towards their car, stopping to chat to friends as they passed through the crowd. Nomalanga wanted to get a message to Themba to tell him that she loved him. She had promised her mother not to write. If she went to Ladysmith, she would not be able to visit him. How could she get Reverend Setuki to give him a message? Suddenly, as they were climbing into the big Mercedes, a plan came into her mind.

'Excuse me, Dada,' she said. 'I must give something to Reverend Setuki for the hospital.' She pulled her purse out of her handbag as though she was going to give some money.

Before Mr Ndlovu could say anything she was hurrying away, back through the crowd. The Reverend was still standing, greeting the last members of the congregation.

'Reverend Setuki,' Nomalanga said, panting for breath, and bowing politely. 'You said you were going to Luthuli hospital this afternoon.'

'Yes, my child,' he replied. 'That is right.'

'Will you be seeing that young man that we prayed for – the one who went into hospital during the night?'

'I expect so.'

'Please would you give him something from me?' Nomalanga asked,

'Certainly, my child,' he said, holding out his hand.

'It . . . it may help him to get better.' She fumbled in her handbag, took out a small object and pressed it into his hand. 'Tell him it's from Nomalanga. That will please him,' she said. She smiled happily. 'Thank you, Reverend Setuki,' she said, and ran off back to the car.

Reverend Setuki looked down at the object in his hand. It was a tiny little harmonica, about four centimetres long. He smiled as he put it in his pocket. Then suddenly he thought, 'I do not know the name of the young man. She forgot to tell me. Oh well . . . I suppose there will only be one young man from Lapula who went into hospital during the night.'

Later that afternoon, when Reverend Setuki arrived at Luthuli hospital, he asked the nurse at enquiries about the young man from Lapula.

'There are two young men,' the nurse replied, looking in her book. 'One is unconscious – the doctor says he is in a critical condition. I'm afraid you will not be able to talk to him. The other is in ward 4 B.'

'Thank you, my child,' said Reverend Setuki.

He found Makalima lying in bed with bandages round his head. He was still in some pain from the beating he had suffered. But it was clear that, in a day or two, he would be well again. He was very pleased to have a visitor – even though he had never been to the Reverend's church, or any other church.

The Reverend sat on the bed and asked how he was feeling, and how he had come to get his injuries. When Makalima told him he had been in a fight, Reverend Setuki shook his head in sorrow.

'You should not fight, my boy,' he said. 'God wants you to love your enemies. God will help you to get better if you promise never to sin again. Will you do that?'

'I will think about it,' Makalima promised.

'Good, good. Do you know a young woman called Nomalanga Ndlovu?'

Makalima burst out laughing – but that made his head ache, so he stopped laughing. Then he said, 'Yes, I know her. I know Mr Ndlovu, Cuthbert and Nomalanga. Yes, I know her.'

'Well she asked me to give this to you,' the Reverend said. He handed the little harmonica to Makalima. 'I shall pray to God to make you well again. Now do not get into any more fights.'

'Yes, Father,' Makalima said. He watched the Reverend leave the ward. Then he looked down in amazement at the small mouth-organ. 'Nomalanga Ndlovu sent me this present? Why?' He laughed and then put it to his mouth and blew. It made his head ache, but it also made him smile.

7

Long-distance Love

Aunt Nonzwakazi lived in Mfulani, a township not far from Ladysmith. She was a very large woman with broad shoulders, big breasts, big arms, big thighs, a big heart and a big voice. Everybody in Mfulani knew Aunt Nonzwakazi. She was the owner of the Amazulu Star – the best shebeen in Ladysmith. Her beer was made from the best sorghum, and the men could drink as much as they liked. They could sing, shout and gamble, but not fight. Any man who started a fight would find the heavy hand of Aunt Nonzwakazi descending on his head. 'If you want to fight,' she would say, 'you can go home and fight with your wife. You do not fight here in my shop. All right?'

Now, although Aunt Nonzwakazi ran the shebeen, she actually lived in a big house on the other side of town, and was the founder of the Church of Jesus – a private church run by a man who called himself Bishop Ngcobo. Long ago, Aunt Nonzwakazi had given him the land and money for his church. So, every Sunday afternoon, the people gathered in the road outside her house, and formed a procession to march to the church.

Aunt Nonzwakazi was, of course, at the head of the procession. She wore a large purple robe, and carried a huge plastic, golden cross on a pole in front of her. Behind her, came the Bishop, in a gold and purple robe, carrying a Bible. Behind him came the choir, in white and purple robes. Finally came the men, women, children and dogs that formed the rest of the congregation. The service lasted from two until five. Then the procession marched back to Aunt Nonzwakazi's house.

Mr Ndlovu had phoned ahead to warn Aunt Nonzwakazi

about their visit. So Aunt Nonzwakazi was not surprised to see the big, black Mercedes outside her house as she headed up the road. She waved the cross at them and, as soon as Bishop Ngcobo had dismissed the choir, she came waddling across, all sweat and dust, to greet them.

'Hullo, my beautiful one!' she said, as she folded Nomalanga into her breasts. 'So you are coming to live with your old Aunt Nonzwakazi. We will do many things together. But Yoh! Yoh! Yoh! You have grown into a beautiful young woman.'

She led the way into her big house and soon had cups of tea or coffee for everybody. Then Mr and Mrs Ndlovu set off on the journey back to Lapula. Aunt Nonzwakazi and Nomalanga stood on the veranda and waved as the car drove off into the distance. Then they went back inside and sat down.

'So, my little angel, tell me about this man that you love. What is he like? Why does your father not like him?' Aunt Nonzwakazi said, flopping herself down into a huge, comfortable armchair.

Nomalanga gasped. 'Who told you that I was in love?' she asked.

'Nobody told me,' Aunt Nonzwakazi replied, laughing. She plumped up a cushion and put it behind her back. 'I don't need to be told by anybody. It is obvious. Your father suddenly decided to send you here to have a holiday with Aunt Nonzwakazi. Why? Because you have fallen in love with a man he does not like!'

Nomalanga stared angrily at Aunt Nonzwakazi, but the old lady looked so cheeky that she could not help laughing. Then, of course, having laughed together, she told the whole story about the Cats' concert, the stabbing of Themba, her visit to the hospital and her hope that, one day, she would see Themba alive and well again.

Suddenly, Aunt Nonzwakazi went silent. She lay back in her chair, with her eyes closed. Nomalanga thought she was ill but she waved her hand for Nomalanga to be still. Then she opened her eyes and sat up.

'Your man is recovering,' she said. 'He is still weak and in pain here.' Aunt Nonzwakazi placed a finger on her large left breast. 'But he is slowly getting better – and he is thinking of you.'

'How can you be sure?' Nomalanga demanded. She thought Aunt Nonzwakazi was trying to cheer her up.

Aunt Nonzwakazi shrugged. 'I don't know how. It just comes into my mind. It happens to me when I hear about people who are in trouble. I thought, "There is a man called Themba Mtuze in a hospital." Then a picture came into my mind of a very big man lying in bed. I saw him lying there, with lots of tubes going in and out of him. There was a nurse standing beside him in a blue uniform. Is that right?' Nomalanga nodded. 'Your Themba is very weak. You must keep on sending love to him. It travels like radio waves. It will find him and help him. But of course, if you do not really love him, he may die. Everything is in your hands, Nomalanga.'

Aunt Nonzwakazi was so serious that Nomalanga felt quite frightened. But Nomalanga decided she would keep on loving Themba whatever happened.

Suddenly they heard the voice of a child calling from outside, 'Mamakhulu! Mamakhulu!' and a small boy came running into the room in great alarm.

'What's the matter, Kodi?' Aunt Nonzwakazi asked.

'Mamakhulu, there is a snake! Come see! Come see!' the small boy cried, grabbing one of her hands and trying to pull her up out of the chair.

'Pull! Pull!' the old lady cried, teasing him. The boy became frantic, as his feet slipped on the floor and he fell down. Laughing loudly, Aunt Nonzwakazi stood up and lifted the boy to his feet. 'Come!' she said. 'Show me this snake.'

Nomalanga went with Aunt Nonzwakazi and Kodi to the

yard at the back of the house. A well-trodden path went through a big clump of thorn bushes to a large building at the back. The boy peered into one of the bushes.

'There! Mamakhulu!' he said, fearfully, holding the old lady's hand. They all peered into the bushes.

A large black millipede was slowly crawling through the grass. Aunt Nonzwakazi bent down and lifted the creature up with finger and thumb and laid it on the pink palm of her hand. It curled itself up and lay quite still.

'There! See, my little boy. It does not want to bite you.' Aunt Nonzwakazi said. 'Hold it so that it can sleep.' She took the child's hand and tipped the millipede on to his palm, holding his hand to steady him. They all watched for a moment as the millipede lay still. Then it tried to uncoil itself. Kodi jumped in fright, ready to drop the millipede, but Aunt Nonzwakazi held his hand firmly.

'Let it go now, child,' she said. 'It wants to find some grass to eat. And, Kodi, that is not a snake. It is a *songololo*. Now go to the kitchen and Mokete will give you an orange. All right, baby?'

The little boy placed the millipede carefully back in the grass and then ran off happily to the kitchen.

'That is one of my wagon-puppies,' Aunt Nonzwakazi said.

'What is a wagon-puppy?' Nomalanga asked.

'I grew up in Ulundi – near to the big road where the wagons went past,' Aunt Nonzwakazi explained. 'One day, I found a puppy lying in the road. Its eyes were still closed. It must have fallen out of the wagon – or perhaps someone threw it out. It was a puppy that nobody wanted. So I looked after it. It was my puppy. I called it my "wagon-puppy". Now that I am living here in Mfulani, I find there are many more wagon-puppies – little boys and girls that nobody wants. Come, I'll show you.'

She led the way down the path to a building at the bottom

of her land. It was a large U-shaped building with dormitories on each side for boys and girls, and a dining-room, kitchen and play-room in the middle. It was, in fact, an orphanage for some twenty to thirty small children. They ranged from small babies of a few weeks old to eight-year-old children. There were eight young women looking after them, and a middle-aged woman, Mrs Lenaka, in charge of them all. The children all seemed to be well-fed and as happy as it is possible for a child to be – that is, a child who has no home, no father and no mother.

'Where do all these children come from?' Nomalanga asked.

Aunt Nonzawakazi shrugged her large shoulders. 'God made men and women to love each other,' she said. 'But He forgot to make them love the fruit of their loving. Some do, some don't. It started when I heard about one of these unwanted children and gave it a place in my home. Two days later, I found another one wrapped in rags, lying on my veranda. Then more and more. What could I do?'

She picked up a fat little baby that came wobbling across the yard to greet her. 'I cannot help it. I love these little ones. The doctor says I can never have children of my own. I used to weep about that. Now I can have as many children as I like. I got the Church of Jesus to form a committee to help me run it. The young girls are all from the choir. Most of the money comes from my profits from The Amazulu Star. Sometimes the men give me money. "Here, Mama," they say to me. "This is for your wagon-puppies." They may give five rands, ten rands, sometimes even twenty rands. Probably some of them are the fathers of these children. Who knows? Who cares?'

Aunt Nonzwakazi put the baby into Nomalanga's arms.

Nomalanga had never before held a baby. At first she was afraid that she would drop it, but it curled up against her breast and started playing with her ear-rings and making little grunting noises of pleasure.

'I thought you might like to take charge of my puppy-house for a few weeks,' Aunt Nonzwakazi said. Nomalanga almost dropped the baby, she had such a fright.

'Mrs Lenaka wants to visit her relations in Bloemfontein,' Aunt Nonzwakazi continued. 'Would you like to try?'

Nomalanga did not know what to say. She was afraid to take on the job, but after working alongside Mrs Lenaka for a few days, she found that she was a natural mother. The children came to her for love and care. The young girls came to her for advice. She did not have to think about it. She was happy looking after the wagon-puppies. The days passed quickly. But at nights, while Aunt Nonzwakazi worked in the shebeen, Nomalanga's thoughts turned to Themba, whom she imagined lying in hospital. Tears rolled down her cheeks as she wondered whether she would ever see Themba again.

8

Show-down

Makalima was told that he would be discharged from hospital. But just as he was getting dressed and ready to leave, Constable Mopani arrived and told him that he was under arrest. So he went from the hospital to the police station and from the police station to the jail. All that he had to show for his adventure, when he stole Rapula's car, were some scars and bruises on his head and body, and the tiny harmonica which the Reverend had given him in hospital. He wished he could see this woman, Nomalanga. He would have liked to thank her.

Meanwhile Themba slowly recovered his strength. The wound, which the knife had made as it passed close to his heart, gradually healed up over the weeks. One Tuesday evening, he opened his eyes and found a young nurse in a blue uniform holding his hand, taking his pulse.

'Where is she?' he asked.

The nurse looked at his large black eyes staring at her. 'So, you are feeling better?' she asked, smiling. 'Do you know where you are?'

Themba's eyes looked around the room. 'No,' he whispered.

'You are in Luthuli hospital,' she said. 'You have been here for some time now.'

'But where is that young woman?' he asked.

'What young woman? You kept saying "Nomalanga! Nomalanga!" while you were lying here. There is nobody called Nomalanga here. The only young woman is me.'

Themba closed his eyes. Now he knew the truth. It was all a dream. Nomalanga had never been to the hospital to see him. He would never see her again – except in his dreams.

They moved him out of intensive care into a general ward. Themba lay watching the people come and go. It seemed to him that somebody had switched off the sun. The world was now a cold, dark place.

After five more days, he was strong enough to get out of bed and walk about. He bought some paper, an envelope and a stamp and wrote a letter to Mrs Ngxolo, telling her that he would be discharged from hospital in a few days. He asked her to come and fetch him.

———— ♥ ————

Mrs Ngxolo and Noluvuyo took a taxi to the hospital. They found Themba in ward 17 C, dressed and ready to go. 'Come! Come, Themba,' Noluvuyo said, excitedly, taking Themba's hand and trying to pull him up. 'The taxi is waiting. I have made a cake for you. Let us go.'

'Leave Themba alone, Noluvuyo,' Mrs Ngxolo said. 'I am sorry, Themba. She has been very excited, ever since we got your letter.'

In the taxi Themba sat in front, with the driver, while Mrs Ngxolo and Noluvuyo sat in the back. The taxi ate up the kilometres and soon they were driving down Twenty-three Street. A grey car was parked outside number 69.

A short, stout, baldheaded man got out of the grey car. He walked across to the window where Themba was sitting. 'Are you Mr Mtuze?' he asked. Themba nodded. 'Ah! I thought I might find you here. I am a lawyer. My name is Gumede. I would like to talk to you about . . .'

'Just a minute! Just a minute!' Mrs Ngxolo shouted from the back. 'This is my taxi. I am not going to pay while you talk.'

Mr Gumede apologised. The taxi driver was paid, and they all went into the house and sat on the chairs around the table. Mr Gumede laid his brief case on the table, opened it and took out some papers.

'I am the lawyer for Mr Cuthbert Ndlovu,' Mr Gumede said. 'The police have accused him of assaulting you on the night of Saturday, 9th February. They want you to appear as a witness in two cases. The first is the case against your friend, Makalima. The second case is against Mr Cuthbert Ndlovu and his friends. Both cases are to come before the magistrate on Wednesday, 27th February. Now I want you to tell me what happened in the bus on that Saturday night . . .'

Themba put his hands firmly on the table and stood up. 'Mr Gumede,' he said. 'I am feeling weak. I have just come out of hospital. I am not in a condition to talk about these things now. If I did feel like it, I would rather talk to the police. But sick as I am, if you do not go out of this house now, I shall pick you up and throw you out, as I did to Cuthbert. Now, kindly go away before I commit another assault.'

Mr Gumede jumped up, grabbed his brief case and ran out of the room.

In the afternoon Sergeant Mogale arrived to talk to Themba. He also wanted to know what Themba had seen and heard when he was in the bus on that Saturday night. Themba wrote out two statements for him. One was about his conversation with Makalima on the afternoon before the concert. The second was about what happened before and during the time that he was assaulted in the bus.

Then Sergeant Mogale said that Themba should go to court at nine o'clock on the 27th. He told Themba that Makalima was in jail, awaiting the trial. The other three, he said, were not in jail. Mr Ndlovu had paid bail for them. He said he did not know anything about Nomalanga.

The days passed until, at last, it was the day for the trial. Mrs Ngxolo and Noluvuyo insisted on going with Themba in a taxi to the magistrates' court in Germiston. They were directed to the back of the court while Themba was directed to the clerk of the court's office. There he was told to wait outside the court until he was called. Some long, wooden benches were provided in the corridor.

Many people walked past him – policemen in uniform, men, women, children, clerks with bundles of files. Then Themba noticed a tall, thin man standing in the corridor, talking to a shorter man. Both men were wearing long black gowns. Themba got up and whispered to a policeman who was passing him. 'Who are those men in black gowns?'

The policeman looked at the two men and then laughed. 'They are lawyers,' he said. 'The tall, thin one is Mr Nkwane. He is the prosecutor. Mr Makalima is accused of stealing a motor car and carrying a dangerous weapon. The prosecutor must try to prove that Mr Makalima is guilty of these things. The other man, the short one, is Mr Motaung. He is the counsel for the defence and will therefore, try to prove that Mr Makalima is not guilty.'

'Where's Makalima?' Themba asked.

'You will see him standing in the dock. The magistrate will ask Makalima to say whether he is guilty or not guilty of stealing the car. Then the witnesses are called. They promise to tell the truth and the two lawyers will ask them questions. The magistrate sits and listens. When everyone has given evidence, he decides if the accused is guilty or not guilty. If he is guilty, then he sentences him. If the magistrate thinks he is not guilty, then the accused is acquitted.'

At that moment, someone called the policeman away. Themba sat down again. The doors were closed. At last, someone shouted, 'Mr Themba Mtuze.' Themba got up and walked into the courtroom.

Another policeman guided him to a platform in the centre of the courtroom. Themba looked around and saw Makalima standing in the dock opposite him.

A policeman stood in front of Themba with a Bible in his hands. He asked Themba to place his hand on it, and to promise to tell the truth, the whole truth and nothing but the truth. He did as he was asked.

The short lawyer, Mr Motaung, walked across to Themba. 'Are you Mr Themba Mtuze of 69 Twenty-third Street, Lapula?' he asked.

'I am,' Themba replied.

'The accused, Makalima, has pleaded guilty to the charge of stealing a car belonging to Mr Rapula Dipale,' the lawyer said. 'Now, I want you to tell me what you saw and heard on Saturday, 9th February. Did the accused come to visit you in your room that day?'

'Yes, he did,' Themba replied.

'Did he tell you he was going to steal a car?'

Themba looked across at Makalima. He did not want to get him into trouble. But he had to tell the truth: he had promised he would. Makalima smiled and nodded. 'Yes,' Themba said.

'Did you agree to go with him?' Mr Motaung asked.

'No,' Themba replied. 'I did not want to go with him. I do not steal other people's things.'

'Did you try to stop him from stealing this car?' Mr Motaung asked.

'Yes,' Themba replied. 'I told him it was foolish. But he said he liked driving smart, fast cars.'

'Did he tell you why he steals cars?'

'Yes,' Themba said. 'He told me that he would never be able to buy one for himself.' Themba looked across at Makalima who was still smiling. 'He said that he liked to drive them, but he did not want to keep them,' Themba explained.

People in the court started laughing. Themba continued. 'Makalima said, he does not have enough money to buy petrol. So, when he has finished driving, he takes the car to the dump.'

'Did he tell you why he does this?'

'Yes,' Themba replied. 'Makalima says, this way everybody is happy. He himself is happy, because he gets a free ride. The owner is happy, because he gets his car back. The police are happy, because they do not have to look for the thief.'

Everybody in the court laughed loudly, but the magistrate held up his hand for silence.

'Thank you, your Honour, I have finished my questions,' Mr Motaung said. He went and sat down, and Mr Nkwane rose and came across to Themba.

'Mr Mtuze,' he said, leaning forward, 'you say that you did not agree to go with the accused when he went to steal the car? Is that correct?'

'Yes,' Themba agreed.

'But the police have told us that they found both of you in that old bus. How do you explain that?'

'It just happened,' Themba replied, shrugging his shoulders. 'I went to a concert in the social centre. My friend, Makalima, stole the car. We both just happened to return to the dump at the same time.'

'Are you one of the Old Block gang?' Mr Nkwane asked.

'No,' Themba said firmly. 'I am not one of them.'

'But you admit that the accused came to your room that day to visit you?'

'Yes,' Themba agreed. 'I have said that we talked that day.'

'I suggest that at other times you went riding with the accused in a stolen car.'

'Never!' Themba replied. 'I have never been in a stolen car.'

'Thank you, Mr Mtuze,' Mr Nkwane said. He turned to the magistrate. 'I too have finished my questions, your Honour,' he said. Then he went and sat down.

Everyone was silent while the magistrate shuffled his papers and wrote things down. At last he stopped and looked around the courtroom.

'Well,' he said, speaking slowly and clearly, so that everyone could hear him. 'We have now heard all the evidence. We have heard how the accused planned to go out that Saturday night to steal a motor car. The witness, Mr Rapula Dipale, has told us how he went with Mr Cuthbert Ndlovu, Mr Takalani Rambula and Mr Vusi Shange to recover the car. We have heard how they found the accused in the car. All three witnesses separately told the same story. So there is no doubt about the verdict. The accused is guilty of theft.'

There were cheers from the back of the courtroom. Themba turned around and saw that Mr and Mrs Ndlovu, Cuthbert, Rapula, Takalani and Vusi were all sitting together. They were clapping and looking very pleased. To his disappointment Nomalanga was not amongst them.

The clerk shouted, 'SILENCE IN THE COURT!' Everyone was quiet and the magistrate continued.

'Before passing sentence, there are other facts that we must take into account,' the magistrate said. 'First, the accused has pleaded guilty to the charge of theft. That is a point in his favour. Secondly, he says he did not really steal the car – he only borrowed it. I must point out that the owner did not give permission. Therefore that is theft. But it is true, he did return the car undamaged. That too is a point in his favour. I shall now pronounce the sentence. The accused will stand.'

A policeman pushed Makalima to his feet.

'I find the accused guilty of the charge of theft,' the magistrate said. Mr Ndlovu and the others started clapping again. The magistrate signalled again for silence.

'In passing sentence,' he said, 'I have taken into account the two points in his favour. I am also taking into account the fact that he was beaten up by the three witnesses. They should be charged with assault. However, they are facing a more serious charge in the next case. So, I will say that they punished him in their own way. Also, he has already spent two weeks in jail. Now, before I sentence the prisoner, I must caution him. If he appears again in this court on the same charge, I will give him the severest sentence allowed by law. For the present, however, he will serve two weeks in jail, or pay a fine of fifty rands.'

There was an angry shout from the back of the courtroom. 'SILENCE IN THE COURT!' the clerk shouted.

Everyone jumped to their feet. The magistrate walked out through the door behind him. Immediately everyone started talking.

Themba went to talk to Makalima. He crossed the floor at the same time as the clerk of the court.

'Do you intend paying the fine, or will you serve the sentence in jail?' the clerk asked Makalima.

'I have no money,' Makalima said, shaking his head sadly. 'I shall have to go to jail for another two weeks.'

'No,' Themba said. 'I have the money. I drew it out this morning from my savings account in the building society.'

'Is there enough for the fine – fifty rands?' the clerk asked. Themba nodded. 'Then come with me, please, to the office. I can give you a receipt,' he said.

They followed him out of the courtroom to his office. Themba pulled out a wad of bank notes from his pocket and counted out five ten-rand notes.

'There is just one condition,' he said to Makalima. 'Before I hand this over, you must promise me that you will not steal any more cars.'

Makalima laughed and slapped Themba on the back. 'I promise,' he said.

Themba handed over the money to the clerk. 'The next case starts at half past two,' the clerk said, as he handed the receipt to Themba. 'As you are both witnesses, I suggest you come back at about a quarter past.'

9

A Test of Love

'Thanks, Themba. I'm now a free man,' Makalima said, as he and Themba walked out of the clerk's office at the magistrates' court. 'I think I need a drink. Come! I know a place where we can get some beers.'

He led the way down some side streets, past the marketplace to a bar. The two men went inside and Themba ordered two beers. When they had been served they sat at a small table.

'Good luck, my old friend,' Makalima said, holding his glass of beer up in the air. 'Thank you for paying my fine. One day I will pay you back.

'I want to sing and dance,' Makalima went on after he'd had a drink. He pulled a small harmonica out of his pocket and started playing. It wasn't a tune. It was just a noise.

'Hey!' Themba said, smiling. 'That is a smart thing. Where did you get it?'

'Yoh! That is a funny story,' Makalima replied. 'A Reverend Minister of the church gave it to me. I don't know his name. He visited me in hospital and gave it to me. He said it was a present from Nomalanga, Mr Ndlovu's daughter. What do you think of that?'

Themba's mouth fell open in surprise. 'Who . . . who did you say?' he asked.

'Nomalanga Ndlovu!' Makalima said, laughing and blowing the tiny mouth-organ.

'Can I look at it?' Themba asked.

Makalima handed over the harmonica, and Themba silently studied it. He held the small, shining instrument in his hand. 'This little thing,' he thought to himself, 'has been held in her hands. She has put her lips on this.' For a moment

Themba felt angry with Makalima for touching it. But, of course, Makalima did not know what had happened to Themba and Nomalanga on that Saturday night.

Themba closed his hand around the harmonica and held it tight. Then he turned to his friend. 'Makalima,' he said, 'that night, at the concert, I met Nomalanga. We sang and played music together. She played a harmonica – a bigger one than this. I played the guitar. I think the Reverend made a mistake.'

'That's tough luck!' Makalima said, holding out his hand. 'It was given to me. I am going to keep it as a souvenir.'

'If you give me this,' Themba said, holding on even more tightly, 'then you need not pay back the fifty rands. What do you say? Is that a deal?'

'Hah!' Makalima laughed. 'It's yours my friend. If it means so much to you, you can have it. I cannot play a tune on it myself. By the way,' he went on. 'I have seen Miss Nomalanga. Yoh! Yoh! Yoh! She's a beautiful woman.'

He laughed and gave Themba a punch on the arm. 'I tell you what, my friend, perhaps that harmonica can play a tune to bring the two of you together. If that happens, then I will give you back that fifty rands for a wedding present. How do you like that?'

Themba laughed, and they shook hands. Then the two friends started telling each other what had happened to them since they had last been together on that terrible Saturday. Suddenly noticing that it was two o'clock, they jumped up and hurried back to the magistrates' court. People were already going into the courtroom, when they arrived. As they were both witnesses, they had to sit in the corridor and wait until they were called.

The trial began and, almost immediately, the policeman shouted, 'Mr Makalima!'

Makalima jumped to his feet and went out through the door to the courtroom.

An hour passed and Themba began to get impatient. What was happening? Why did they not call him? Suddenly the door to the courtroom opened and people started coming out – Mr Nkwane, Mr Gumede, various others and then Makalima.

'What's happening?' Themba asked.

'The magistrate has decided to have a tea-break,' Makalima said. 'Of course, they all get tea – the lawyers and officials. But there's no tea or coffee for us.'

'What about the case?' Themba asked. 'What has happened?'

Makalima frowned and said, 'Those boys from the New Block gang, Cuthbert, Takalani and Vusi look guilty to me but they have pleaded not guilty. They say they didn't assault you; they only assaulted me, because I stole the car. They say that, after they took the knife away from me, they carried me to the bus. I was barely conscious – which is all quite true.'

'So, what do they say happened next?' Themba asked.

'Hah! This is where I think they start telling lies,' Makalima said. 'They say they heard somebody moving at the end of the bus. So they dropped the knife, ran out and hid in the bushes. Then they saw you go into the bus and heard you fall on the floor. When they heard the police siren, they ran to the beer hall in Five Street. They say they think some drug-addicts stabbed you with the knife. The trouble is this,' Makalima prodded Themba on the chest with one finger, 'their story sounds true. But I still think one of them stabbed you.'

Everybody started going back to the courtroom, and everything was much as it had been before, except that Cuthbert, Takalani and Vusi were now the accused standing together in dock. Cuthbert and Vusi – both tall men – were dressed smartly in suits. Short, fat little Takalani stood between them in an old jacket and trousers. He did not look at all happy. And instead of Mr Motaung, Mr Gumede was now the counsel for the defence. He glared at Themba as he entered the witness box.

Themba wanted to turn round to look at the people in the court, but the policeman brought the Bible for him to swear to tell the truth, and then the prosecutor started questioning him immediately.

Themba had to tell the court how he'd fought Cuthbert at the Cats' concert, then how he had walked from Mr Ndlovu's house to the old bus in the dump. Finally, he told of how he had heard someone groaning in the bus, went in and saw Makalima lying there.

'Then I heard someone moving behind me,' Themba said. 'I started to turn round, to see who it was. But suddenly I felt a sharp pain in my back. Then I fell down. I knew nothing more until I woke up in hospital.'

The prosecutor then brought across a knife, which was lying on a table in front of the magistrate.

'Mr Mtuze,' he said. 'This is the knife that was used to stab you. It belonged to your friend, Makalima. He has admitted that he carried it with him. He says it was taken away from him, by one of the accused, namely, Takalani. You were in the bus. All three of these men had good reason to hate you. You had fought with their leader, Cuthbert Ndlovu, that same night. Do you not think it is possible that one of them may have stabbed you in revenge for what you did to Cuthbert?'

Before Themba could answer, Mr Gumede jumped to his feet.

'Objection, your Honour. My learned friend, the prosecutor, is asking the witness what he thinks. That is not evidence.'

'You are right, Mr Gumede,' the magistrate said. 'We are here to listen to the facts, Mr Nkwane. We want to know what actually happened, not what the witness thinks may have happened. Is that clear?'

Mr Nkwane bowed. 'Yes, your Honour,' he said. He turned back to Themba. 'We believe that one of the three accused stabbed you, while the other two looked on. I want you to think carefully before you answer this question. Are you quite, quite sure, Mr Mtuze, that you did not see one of the three accused, standing somewhere in the bus, perhaps on one side, or behind you?'

There was absolute silence in the court. Themba realised that if he said the name of any one of the three, that man would probably go to jail. They all looked at him in fear. The power was in his hands, but he had promised to tell the truth.

'I saw nobody,' he said.

A great sigh went up from everyone in the court. Then the magistrate held up his hand for silence. 'Have you anything more to say, Mr Nkwane?' he asked.

'Nothing, your Honour,' Mr Nkwane said.

'And you, Mr Gumede?'

Mr Gumede looked very pleased with himself. 'No questions, your Honour,' he said. 'My learned friend has proved my case for me.' Somebody in the court laughed, others cheered.

'I am going to adjourn the court for twenty minutes,' the magistrate said. 'I want to consider my verdict.'

———— ♥ ————

Themba and Makalima sat together on the benches in the corridor, outside the courtroom.

'What do you think will happen now?' Themba asked.

'Well, there's nobody else to give evidence,' Makalima said. 'There's no evidence to prove who stabbed you. If you had said that you saw one of them coming behind you, then it would be different. I think the magistrate will find them not guilty. They may well go free.'

Suddenly a policeman shouted that everyone must go

back into court. Themba and Makalima sat on one of the benches in the front of the court. Everyone stood up when the magistrate entered. Then he made an announcement.

'The prosecutor has told me that he has another witness. I have given permission for the new witness to give evidence. Call your witness, Mr Nkwane.'

Then they heard the policeman call out, 'Miss Nomalanga Ndlovu!' The door opened and Nomalanga walked towards the centre of the courtroom. To Themba it seemed as if the sun had started shining.

As she walked past him she bowed her head and smiled at him. He saw again how her lips curled up at the corners when she smiled. It only lasted a second, but it was enough to make his heart start beating faster and his throat to swell so that he could not speak.

Nomalanga was dressed in a plain dark-green dress in a fashionable cut. With her head held high, she looked dignified, cool and confident.

Mr Ndlovu called out from the back of the court, 'Nomalanga! What are you doing, Nomalanga?' A policeman immediately went across and told him to be quiet.

The magistrate looked up. 'If you cannot keep silent, sir, you will have to leave the court,' he said.

Nomalanga was then sworn in and Mr Nkwane approached her to question her. 'Miss Ndlovu,' he said. 'I only know that you say that you have further evidence you wish to give. Is that correct?'

'Yes,' Nomalanga said. She spoke loudly and clearly, so that everyone could hear.

'Then would you like to tell the court in your own words what information you have that may be of interest?'

People in the court moved about in their seats. They wanted to see the witness. Then there was absolute silence. Everyone waited tensely to hear what this beautiful, well-dressed young woman had to say.

'On that Saturday night,' Nomalanga said clearly. 'I met Mr Themba Mtuze for the first time. We sang together at the concert. There was a fight between my brother and Mr Mtuze. Then we went to my home. Mr Mtuze left me in the road outside our house. I went straight to bed. Later, my brother came and woke me up. It was about five o'clock the next morning.'

This time it was Cuthbert who tried to interrupt her. 'No, Nomalanga,' he said. He looked at her earnestly and shook his head.

Nomalanga looked across the court, directly at Cuthbert. 'I must tell the truth,' she said. 'When I have finished, I will explain why I have done so.' She turned back to Mr Nkwane. 'As I have said, my brother woke me at five o'clock in the morning. These are his words, as I remember them. "There is trouble. I think the police are looking for me. It's the gang from the Old Block – Themba, your new friend." Then he told me about the theft of Rapula's car, and how they had caught and beaten Mr Makalima, and taken away his knife. He said that Takalani was the one who took the knife, and carried it with him into the bus.'

'It is lies! It is all lies!' Takalani shouted.

'Be quiet!' said the clerk of the court.

Nomalanga now spoke very softly. The people at the back of the court had to strain to hear her. 'My brother told me then that Takalani had stabbed Mr Mtuze. I was very frightened when he told me that. That is all my evidence.'

There was silence in the court after Nomalanga had finished speaking. It was clear to everyone now that the three men had been proved guilty.

Mr Nkwane looked up at Nomalanga. 'You said, Miss Ndlovu, that you would explain to the court why you had decided to come forward with this evidence.'

'Yes,' Nomalanga said. 'Things are changing today. If we want to build a better future for our children we need to tell the truth and live in peace. For years and years people have been fighting and telling lies because they belong to different tribes, or different political parties. They have been fighting because their skins are different colours. They have been fighting because some are rich, others poor. This is not the way to have a happy, peaceful, prosperous country. Now we must start new customs in our country. So I decided I must tell the truth.'

The magistrate leaned forward. He was interested in what this young woman was saying. 'What do you think people should do then, Miss Ndlovu?' he said. 'There has been fighting here, in the town of Lapula. What should people do to stop it?'

'Many of the young men in Old Block are unemployed and have nothing to do,' Nomalanga said. 'The council should help them. It could at least do something like building a football field. That would give work to some of these young men in Old Block who have got no jobs. And, instead of fighting, the young men of New Block and Old Block could play football.'

There was great clapping and cheering from the people in the court, until the magistrate held up his hand for silence.

'Thank you, Miss Ndlovu,' he said. 'I hope that the Lapula Town Council will take note of what you have suggested. Now, we must get back to the case in court. I will sum up the evidence.'

The magistrate went over all the facts. Then he went on, 'It is clear that the accused had a motive for wanting to attack Mr Mtuze. They had admitted that they were in the area where the crime occurred. And they have admitted that one of them took the knife away from Mr Makalima Bongela. They have said that there was someone else at the bottom end of the bus, but there is no evidence of this. Mr Mtuze did not see anyone coming towards him from the bottom end, and the police did not see anyone coming out of the bus. The evidence we have suggests that they were the only people there when Mr Mtuze was stabbed. However, on this evidence alone we cannot prove that they were guilty of assaulting Mr Mtuze.

'So far, I have said nothing about the evidence which we have just heard from Miss Ndlovu,' he went on. 'It was brave of her to tell us what she did. Probably some people in Lapula think she should have kept quiet. They would like to punish her. But she has given her reasons for telling the truth, and I believe she is right. Her evidence provides proof that Mr Takalani Rambula did in fact stab Mr Mtuze, and that his two friends, Cuthbert Ndlovu and Vusi Shange, assisted him by helping him to escape, and lying to protect him.'

The magistrate shuffled his papers. Then he said, 'I find the accused, Takalani Rambula, guilty of stabbing Mr Mtuze. He will either serve a sentence of six months' imprisonment, or pay a fine of six hundred rands. I find Cuthbert Ndlovu and Vusi Shange guilty of being accessories to the crime. They are both sentenced to two months' imprisonment or they must pay a fine of two hundred rands each.'

'Silence in the court!' shouted the clerk, as the magistrate rose to his feet. Everyone stood up as the magistrate walked out. Then there was pandemonium. Everyone started shouting, talking and waving to each other. Mr Ndlovu shouted again, and shook his fist.

Themba jumped to his feet and ran across to the witness box, where Nomalanga was sitting. Her eyes were shining with love and happiness.

'Themba,' she said. 'Are you well now?' But before he could answer, she grabbed his hand. 'Come!' she said, 'We must get out of here. We have to talk.'

She held on to his hand and led him out of the court, through the door used by the witnesses. They went out, to a small Volkswagen Beetle that was parked in the street. She pulled a key out of her handbag and opened the passenger door.

'Get in!" she said briefly. She swung the car round in the street and headed off into the town. They were on their way before anyone else had even come out of the courthouse.

10

Reunited

Nomalanga drove fast through the streets of Germiston. Themba was overwhelmed. He felt breathless. He did not know where they were going. All that he wanted to say was, 'Nomalanga, I love you.' He wanted to put his arms around her. He wanted to cover her face with kisses. But he could not do any of these things because she was driving so fast.

Nomalanga looked sideways at him and smiled. Then the words came flowing out of her mouth. It was as though somebody had turned on a tap. 'The car belongs to my Aunt Nonzwakazi,' she said. 'I'll tell you about her later. But first tell me, are you better? When did you get out of hospital? I thought you were dying when I saw you there in the hospital. But Aunt Nonzwakazi said you were getting better. Of course, my mother wrote to me from home, but she did not give me any news of you. My father and mother would not let me write to you. I had no news of you. Oh, Themba. I was so worried about you . . .'

Suddenly Nomalanga drew the car into a parking space and switched off the engine. Then she threw her arms around his neck. In a moment she was covering his cheeks with kisses. She was laughing and crying at the same time. The tears were running down her cheeks, but her eyes and mouth were full of laughter. Themba could not speak because, every time he opened his mouth, she planted her lips on his. At last she stopped for breath and moved her head away from his face.

Her arms were still about his neck when she said, 'Themba, man, I love you.' She put her head on one side, smiling at him. 'Do you love me?'

Themba turned to face her. He put his arms clumsily

around her shoulders. There was not much room in that little Volkswagen for a big man like him. Yet it seemed to him that this little car was the whole world.

'Nomalanga, my dear, dear woman,' he said. 'I love you. You must know that I love you. I have loved you from the moment we met at the Cats' concert. I have been so afraid that I would never see you again. Now . . . now here you are . . .' The words would not come out. He drew her towards him and held her tightly. He buried his face in the soft flesh of her neck.

Suddenly, Nomalanga let go. She gave him a quick, light kiss, like a bird pecking at an apple. 'Come!' she said. 'We have much to talk about.'

They drove through Germiston until they came to the outskirts. The road passed through a grove of bluegum trees to a line of small shops beside the road. One of these was a two-storey building, with Ramona Cafe on one side and Sammy's Supermarket on the other.

'Come!' Nomalanga said. She stopped the car and removed the keys. 'I have something to show you.'

Between the two shops was a plain wooden door. Nomalanga fumbled with her keys and then opened the door. Inside was a passageway with a large old, wooden cupboard. The passage led to some concrete steps. Nomalanga led the way up the steps to a landing, with doors leading off on each side.

She opened the door on the right. 'Welcome to the SHINSA office!' she said. 'This is the place where big plans are made.'

'What is SHINSA?' Themba asked, looking around him.

In the centre of the room were several chairs facing each other around a low round table. On each side of this there were desks and tables, littered with files and papers, a telephone, a typewriter, a small cupboard, a tray of mugs and an electric kettle. There was a handbasin, and towels. A large fire extinguisher hung above the handbasin.

The door on the other side of the landing opened and Aunt Nonzwakazi entered. 'So you have brought the man back?' she said. She was dressed in a huge, bright orange and yellow kaftan dress, which fell away to her feet like a tent. On her head she wore a yellow scarf and a big, red brooch, mounted in gold with stiff yellow bristles spread out on top like a plume of feathers.

'Themba, this is my Aunt Nonzwakazi,' Nomalanga said.

'And is this the man himself – Themba Mtuze?' Aunt Nonzwakazi asked. To Themba's surprise and embarrassment, the big lady threw one arm around his neck, pulled his face towards her and planted a fat kiss on each cheek. Then she released him. 'Yes,' she said, looking at him, with her head on one side. 'He looks just like I saw him.'

'When you were ill in hospital,' Nomalanga explained, 'Aunt Nonzwakazi visited you in her mind. She can see and hear things in the spirit world.'

'You did not see me, Themba, but I saw you,' Aunt Nonzwakazi said. She filled the kettle from the tap in the handbasin. 'It's all right, young man,' she said over her shoulder. 'I can only link with people when they are suffering, either in their body or their mind.'

She switched on the kettle and then signalled for Themba to sit in one of the chairs in the middle of the room. She and Nomalanga sat facing him. 'You see,' she said, without stopping, 'when your spirit suffers, you give off waves of pain. They are like radio waves. They go out into the air. Anybody who is near you, who loves you, will know this. But psychic people can pick up these waves from faraway. It is like tuning in a television set or a radio set. I can see and hear people talking inside my head. Of course, it is not clear, as it is on tv or radio. Sometimes I only hear the voices. But if the person is in great trouble, then I can see them and hear them. That is how I saw you and heard you in the hospital.'

Themba was enthralled. He had heard of such things but had never come across it himself. 'Do you mean, all the time, even now while you are talking to me, you are getting these pictures and voices?' he asked.

'No, no,' Aunt Nonzwakazi said, laughing. 'I have to switch on. That's what I call it. I sit down quietly and close my eyes, and I close my mind to everything else. I don't think about anything, except the person who is suffering.'

'But you did not know me,' Themba said. 'How could you think about me?'

'Ah, yes. But there was somebody else who knew you and loved you.' She turned and pointed her finger at Nomalanga. 'This child here was my link,' she said. 'It was Nomalanga's love which gave me the right wavelength to allow me to get through to you. Then I saw you in hospital, with a nurse standing beside you. There were bottles hanging up next to the bed with tubes going into your arm and your mouth. The nurse was wearing a blue uniform. Three times I came to you. Then you got better and I knew the pain had gone away.'

The kettle started boiling. 'You make coffee, Nomalanga,' Aunt Nonzwakazi said. 'I want to talk to this big man, Themba.' She put her hand on Themba's knee and looked straight into his eyes. 'Did you tell the truth at the trial?' she said.

'Yes,' Themba answered simply. 'I did not think that lies would help me.'

'Good! Good! If this country of ours is to become a new land of hope, then that is what people must do – tell the truth,' Aunt Nonzwakazi said, thumping the arm of her chair with her fist. 'Were the three from the New Block gang found guilty?' she asked.

'Yes,' Themba replied. 'And when Nomalanga came, she

changed everything.' Suddenly he found that he could not talk. His throat had swelled up. He remembered how Nomalanga had come into the court like a ray of sunshine.

'Yes, I told her she must give evidence,' Aunt Nonzwakazi said, laughing. 'You didn't want to go to court, did you, my little bird?' Aunt Nonzwakazi looked up, as Nomalanga came across the room, carrying mugs of coffee.

'Cuthbert didn't like me giving evidence but I felt I had to tell the truth,' Nomalanga said.

'What about your father? What did he say?' Aunt Nonzwakazi asked.

'I did not see him.' Nomalanga slipped her small, soft hand into Themba's large firm hand. 'Themba and I left before my father could speak to me.'

Aunt Nonzwakazi stood up, smiling down at the two lovers. 'I don't think you two want to sit here listening to an old woman talking. Why don't you take your cups of coffee through to the flat? I have work to do here. I will come through and join you for supper at, say, six o'clock. You will find some stewing meat in the fridge, Nomalanga. And there is samp and beans in the tins on the shelf. Will you cook those for me?'

Nomalanga stood up. 'Come!' she said. Themba followed her across the landing.

'This is the SHINSA flat,' Nomalanga said. 'Aunt Nonzwakazi, and other people, use this when they are in Egoli. There's a bedroom and bathroom over there, and there's a little kitchen-dining room. And there's lots of room to sit and talk over here.'

Themba did not need another invitation. He put down his mug and turned to face her. She smiled happily and walked straight into his arms. He buried his face in her soft shoulder and could smell the sweet smell of her warm skin. Then he drew away to look at her. There were the two wide, brown eyes, like two deep pools of water, looking up at him. There was the curved, smiling mouth, waiting to be kissed. There was the beautiful face that he had seen so often in his dreams.

Nomalanga looked up at Themba. She saw again his broad face, his strong cheek-bones, his confident smile, his clear, wide eyes. She knew inside herself that this was a man she could trust. This was a man who said what he did, and did what he said. He was a true man – a man to love and a man to be loved by. Here, in his arms, she felt safe. She waited with longing for his kiss.

Standing there together, pressed against each other, they kissed and kissed. Then they sat on the couch and kissed some more. At last, breathless from the many kisses, Nomalanga turned away. 'Tell me what happened to you when you were in hospital,' she said.

Once they started talking, they could not stop. There was so much to tell. They sat together on the couch and talked about what had happened since that Saturday night, when they parted outside Nomalanga's home. They were just starting to talk about the jobs they did, when Aunt Nonzwakazi came bursting into the room.

'How is the supper coming on?' she asked in her loud voice as she came through the door. Then she saw them sitting together, with their arms around each other. 'Just as I thought,' she said. 'Young people today only think about kissing and making love.'

Nomalanga stood up and laughed. It sounded like the laughing water of a mountain stream, Themba thought.

'In your day, Aunt Nonzwakazi, when you were young, didn't the young people kiss?'

'Hah!' Aunt Nonzwakazi replied, smiling. 'Of course we did. But we did not know about SHINSA. Anyway, I had better SHINSA myself some supper.'

'What is this SHINSA?' Themba asked, turning to Nomalanga. 'You both keep saying SHINSA. I have never heard of it.'

Nomalanga laughed again and walked across to the kitchen. 'Sorry, Aunt Nonzwakazi,' she said. 'I forgot to cook the food. We were too busy kissing and talking. I will cook the food and you sit here and tell Themba about SHINSA.'

'You are a good girl, my Nomalanga. It is true, I am tired. You cook the supper. Themba and I will talk about SHINSA.' She turned to Themba. 'Before I tell you about SHINSA, I want to know more about you. What do you do?'

'I have no job,' Themba replied. 'I was working for a builder in Germiston. I was a bricklayer but, while I was in hospital, my boss gave my job to another man. So now I have no job. Well, I went to Fort Hare to study. I wanted to become a civil engineer – to build dams, roads and bridges.' Themba's face lit up, as he said this. 'My uncle, who lived in Port Elizabeth, had a lorry. One day, when I was a small boy, he took me with him. We stopped near the bridge at Storms River. Have you ever seen that bridge?' He turned round to look at Nomalanga. He was very excited.

'It is a most wonderful thing,' he said. 'There is a big crack in the mountain, where the river has pushed through. The rocks go straight down on each side. The gap is about five hundred metres wide. Across this gap is a thin bridge made of steel and concrete. As you look at it from the side, it looks like a thin thread going from one side to the other. I saw cars and big lorries, full of bricks, petrol and milk all going across this bridge at the same time. I thought, it will break. It is too much. They are too heavy. But the bridge did not break. It did not even move. Then I said to myself, one day I will build a bridge like that.'

Themba shrugged his shoulders, 'But it was a dream. It will never happen. I wanted to become a civil engineer. That was why I went to Fort Hare. But they did not teach Civil Engineering there. The professor said I should study Mathematics and Physics. So I did that and I was just ready to take the exams when there was a strike. They closed the college, and when it re-opened, I did not have enough money to start again.'

'Would you know how to make a football field level?' Aunt Nonzwakazi asked.

'Yes,' Themba replied. He turned around to look at Nomalanga. 'This is what Nomalanga was talking about in court.' He turned back to Aunt Nonzwakazi. 'Of course I know what to do, if you give me a dumpy level and a bulldozer.'

'All right, you can have a dumpy level,' Aunt Nonzwakazi said, laughing. 'But you cannot have a bulldozer. That costs too much money. Would you be able to organise a gang? You would need lots of men using spades and wheelbarrows and donkey-carts. That is how you would have to clear the bush at the dump to make the ground level.'

'Are you offering me a job?' Themba asked. He started laughing. He could picture in his mind the people all working together, as they used to work in Ntselemanzi – the village where he grew up in the Ciskei. 'It would take lots of men,' he said. 'There would be lots of talking, singing, laughing. It would take a long time, but it would get done, and the people would be proud of it. That is how they did things in the old days.'

'And that is how they are going to do things in the new South Africa,' Aunt Nonzwakazi said. 'With people, talking, laughing and working together to build things for themselves. That is the SHINSA way.'

'Please, please, tell me what is this SHINSA that you and Nomalanga keep on talking about,' Themba said.

'SHINSA is spelt S.H.I.N.S.A,' Aunt Nonzwakazi said. 'It stands for "Self Help In New South Africa". It is something I have started. I will tell you how it happened. One day, at

Mfulani, a man from England came to see me. His name was Mr Evans. He wanted to see my house for wagon-puppies.'

'She means her orphanage,' Nomalanga explained. 'She has an orphanage for little children. It is a very happy place.'

'Shut up Nomalanga!' Aunt Nonzwakazi said, laughing. 'It is my turn to talk to Themba. You have had your chance. As I was saying, this man, Mr Evans from England, came to see me. He had heard about my orphanage. He wanted to know how I organised it, where I got the money from, things like that.

'Mr Evans belongs to an organisation in England called "Technical Aid". It helps people in poor countries to help themselves. We talked for a long time about the problems of poverty. This man said, if I would start a self-help organisation here, they would help us.'

'So, now you have lots of money from England,' Themba said. 'And you are offering me the job of making a football field in Lapula. How much money have you got?'

'No, no,' Aunt Nonzwakazi replied. 'It is not quite like that. This organisation in England does not give away money. They only help by sending experts to advise. They have scientists, engineers, doctors and teachers who work for them. They will advise us, if we need advice. They have worked out clever ways in which people can make dams and roads, bridges and buildings. They use cheap materials and the muscles of lots of people.'

'And if people want to use their muscles, they have to eat lots of food,' Nomalanga said. 'The food is ready now. Come and eat. You can go on talking while we eat.'

There was a plain wooden table, with benches on each side, in the kitchen corner. Nomalanga had laid out basins of water for washing their hands, and placed the pots of food in the centre.

'I suppose you two young people will want to sit as close

together as possible. You two sit together on that bench. I'll sit here,' Aunt Nonzwakazi said.

'I think I have never been happier in my life,' Themba thought, as he sat down.

11

A Promise

Nomalanga, Themba and Aunt Nonzwakazi were sitting together at the table in the SHINSA flat, eating their supper. In front of each was a plate of samp and beans, with lumps of meat and a thick gravy. Themba enjoyed sitting next to Nomalanga. Sometimes their arms touched, and their smiling eyes met.

'Nomalanga,' Themba said. 'You told the magistrate in court that you thought the Lapula Town Council should clear the land at the dump, and build a football field. But Aunt Nonzwakazi says the SHINSA idea is different: the people should do it. Which is right?'

'Nawh, awh ta peepa.' Aunt Nonzwakazi was trying to talk, but her mouth was full of hot samp and meat. She tapped her cheek and swallowed quickly. Then she said, 'No, all the people in Lapula must get a chance to say what they think. They are the ones who must do the work. So there must be a general meeting for everybody. That is what the chiefs used to do in the old days. They held a big *indaba*. But,' Aunt Nonzwakazi banged her fist on the table, so that the plates, knives and spoons bounced in the air, 'in the days of the chiefs, only the men could speak. Now, in the new South Africa, we women must also go to the meetings and speak.'

'Yah! Yah!' Nomalanga said excitedly. 'It is time that the men let the women say what they think. We cannot always sit quietly in the corner and say, "Yes, my boss," to everything they say.'

'But do you think the Lapula Town Council will call such a meeting?' Themba asked. 'They always decide things by themselves in the council.'

'I will try to get my father to call such a meeting,' Nomalanga said. 'If he refuses, then we must try to organise it ourselves. Can we do that, Aunt Nonzwakazi?'

'It is up to you, Themba, to take on this job. I'll tell you how to do it. First you will need to have a place where you can call a general meeting. You will have to approach the Reverend Setuki or the school headmaster and see if they would let you use the church or the school as a meeting-place. Then you must call a general meeting and invite lots of ordinary people from both the Old Block and the New Block. We could print some posters for you, here in the SHINSA office. These posters would inform people about the meeting and could be put up all over Lapula.'

'WHAT DO WE DO WITH THE DUMP?' Nomalanga shouted. 'That is what we will print on our posters.' Her eyes were alight and shining with joy. She threw her arms around Themba's neck. 'This is going to be exciting, isn't it? What next, Aunt?'

'Then, you invite some of the local people to speak at the meeting. But you, Themba, will be the main speaker. You will have to tell the people how you are going to turn the dump into a football field. If people like the idea, then you could form a committee to help you. The committee could take the names and addresses of those who wanted to help in making the football field. They could organise those people into working gangs – a different one each weekend. You would have to tell the workers that they should bring spades, picks, axes, saws, wheelbarrows, donkey-carts – anything that could be used for chopping down the bush and levelling the ground. But, of course, this will all come later.'

'That sounds fine,' Themba said. 'But I cannot start work unless the council gives permission.'

'Don't worry,' Aunt Nonzwakazi said. 'If enough people support the idea, the council will agree. SHINSA!' she shouted, raising her fist in the air, as if she was shouting freedom. Nomalanga stood up.

'It's time I took Themba home,' she said. 'And it is time I went home to my father and mother. They saw me in court this afternoon. They will be wondering where I am. Mama will be worried. May I take the car, Aunt Nonzwakazi? I will phone you tomorrow.'

A few minutes later, Themba and Nomalanga left. They were alone together once more. As they were passing through the grove of blue-gum trees, Themba said, 'Please stop a minute, Nomalanga. Pull off the road.'

Nomalanga looked across at him. The light from the dashboard showed up the strong line of his jaw, and his firm mouth. He was looking out into the darkness with a very serious expression on his face. She steered the car into a sandy track at the side of the road, braked and switched off the engine.

'So you want some more kisses?' she asked.

'Not kisses,' he replied in his deep bass voice. 'I want the answer to three important questions. One, do you love me?'

'I told you I love you,' she replied, putting her arm around his neck, but he pushed her away.

'Next question,' he said. 'Do you love anybody else?'

Nomalanga laughed. 'Old Mr Jealous,' she said. 'What are you worried about?'

'Just tell me,' he said. 'Is there anyone else?'

'Well, I know our lawyer, Mr Gumede, loves me and my parents want me to marry him, but I do not love him. You are the only man I love,' she replied.

'A third question, then. Will you marry me?'

Nomalanga burst out laughing. 'WHAT???' she said. She hugged him. 'You funny man. I never thought I would hear a man asking me such a question. You mean that you want to pay my father *lobola*? Have you got enough cows to buy me?'

Themba felt embarrassed. 'No,' he said, awkwardly. 'I don't mean *lobola*, and all those old customs. I mean making promises to each other. In the court today you and I both told the truth. I want to tell you I will always love you and I want to live with you for the rest of my life. I will love no other woman. That is the truth. And I want you to say the same truthfully to me.'

He turned and faced her. 'You see, Nomalanga,' he began, frowning. Nomalanga watched the muscles rippling in his shoulders, as he moved his arms around her. 'I lost you,' he said. 'I thought I would never find you again. Now I have found you, and I do not want to lose you ever again. That is why I want you to promise to marry me.'

Nomalanga was not laughing now. She looked into his eyes for a moment. His eyes looked steadily into hers. Then she took his face in her hands and held it, so that she could kiss him firmly on the mouth.

Still holding his face, she said, 'If that is what you want, my dear Themba, then that is what we shall do. But first, I must tell my father and mother. I shall tell them tonight.'

Then she put her arms around his neck and they kissed and held each other for a long time. At last she pushed him away.

'Let us meet at the SHINSA flat tomorrow afternoon, after I have finished work at five o'clock,' she said. 'I will tell you then what they say.'

Nomalanga started the engine, drove to Twenty-three Street and dropped Themba at number 69. The Ngxolo family gave him a noisy welcome – especially Noluvuyo, who rushed up to him and took his hand. Nomalanga saw this and frowned slightly, but she soon put it out of her mind as Themba turned and waved to her.

Nomalanga parked the blue Volkswagen in the drive outside her home and let herself in through the front door.

Mr and Mrs Ndlovu were watching television and looked around when they heard her enter.

'So, you have come home?' Mr Ndlovu said. 'Where have you been, Nomalanga?'

'I have been with Aunt Nonzwakazi,' Nomalanga said. 'She has an office and a small flat outside Germiston.'

'An office and a flat? Here in Egoli? I didn't know that,' Mrs Ndlovu said. But Mr Ndlovu was not interested in Aunt Nonzwakazi, nor her office and flat.

'We saw you going off with that man, Themba Mtuze,' he said. 'What for?'

'I love that man, Dada,' Nomalanga replied. She looked straight at her father. 'I love him and he has asked me to marry him.'

'*Marry* you?' Mr Ndlovu said the word, as though he had never heard it before.

'Oh, yes,' Mrs Ndlovu said excitedly. 'Nomalanga is going to get MARRIED. You do want to get married in church, don't you? I know where we can buy a beautiful white, silk dress for you. And you will carry flowers, of course. I thought red roses would be pretty.' She paused, then she went on. 'But we think you should marry Mr Gumede, don't we?' She turned to her husband.

'I don't want to talk about Nomalanga marrying anybody – not tonight,' Mr Ndlovu said firmly. 'We'll talk about it in the morning.' At that moment Cuthbert came in.

'Oh!' Nomalanga said in surprise. 'I thought the magistrate sent you to prison.'

'Don't be so foolish!' her father replied angrily. 'You don't think I would let my son go to prison, do you? And, if you had kept quiet, the magistrate would not have found him guilty. Anyway, I paid the fine, so he is free.'

'What about the other two – Takalani and Vusi?' Nomalanga asked. 'Did you pay their fines too?'

'No, of course not,' Mr Ndlovu replied. 'It will do them good to spend a few months in prison. In future they will be more careful. Now, I am going to bed.' He walked out of the room.

12

Joy and Pain

The next morning Themba was lying in bed, deep in thought, when he heard Noluvuyo knocking at his door. 'Can I come in? I have something important to tell you,' she said.

'All right,' Themba replied. He got up and dressed quickly. Then he opened the door. Noluvuyo walked in and sat on his chair.

'Themba,' she said. 'Please can you come to the school today? I told our teacher about you. He, and some of the girls, heard you singing at the concert. Then the teacher told the headmaster. And, of course, everybody knows about the court case. On Tuesday, the headmaster told me he wants you to come and talk to all the children. You see, on Thursdays, we always have school assembly.'

'What does he want me to talk about?' Themba asked, smiling at the girl. He had never been asked to talk at a school assembly before.

'Anything,' Noluvuyo replied, laughing. 'It doesn't matter what you talk about. It will all be wonderful. You can tell them about the court case, or about when you were in hospital. Or you can play the guitar or sing – anything. Please, Themba. Please.'

'When?' Themba asked.

'This morning, at half past eight,' Noluvuyo said.

Themba looked at the alarm clock that stood on his table.

'There isn't enough time,' he said.

'Yes, there is. You can use Dada's bicycle. He never uses it. I'll ask him.' Noluvuyo jumped up before Themba could stop her, and ran out of the door.

A moment later Mr Ngxolo appeared at the door. 'Noluvuyo says you want to borrow my bike,' he said. 'That's all right, Themba. I never use it. In fact, I want to sell it. If you know anyone who wants to buy it, they can have it for twenty rands.'

'Twenty rands? All right, Mr Ngxolo, I'll buy it,' Themba said.

While he'd been lying in bed, Themba had been thinking about this new job. He had realised that, if he was going to organise this self-help project, there would have to be some changes. Now he would not have to catch the train to Germiston every day. He would no longer be working with bricks and cement – not at first, anyway. However, he would be working with people – and talking to them. People were like bricks that you could build into an institution. And talk was like the cement that bound them together. So he would need to talk to people. And he would need something like a bicycle for getting around the town, from house to house, street to street.

Then he would have to make speeches at meetings. That was something he had never done before. So he might as well start now, by talking to the schoolchildren. He would tell them about making a football field on the dump. Then they would go home and tell their parents. The quickest way of getting news around a town was to tell the children, he thought.

He lit his small oil stove and boiled water for coffee. Then he ate some bread, drank his coffee and set off on his new bicycle for Lapula Secondary School.

The headmaster was standing outside his office when Themba arrived. He was a short, stout little man with a black moustache. He took Themba around to the back of the school, where the children were all standing at the edge of the playground, facing a sloping bank. The headmaster led the way up some steps to the top of the bank. Then he turned to face the children.

'Children,' he said. 'This is Mr Themba Mtuze.'

Immediately all the children chanted. 'Goood mooooorning Meeeestah Mtuuuze.'

Themba was embarrassed. He nodded. 'Good morning,' he said. 'It was kind of your headmaster to invite me to speak to you. I have some important news for you. We live here in Old Block. Over there are people living in New Block. Do you like those people?'

'No!!!!!!' shouted the children.

'Well, I have to tell you this. Those people are the same as we are. Some people say we are enemies. I say we should be friends. Instead of fighting, the people of New Block and Old Block should work together to make Lapula a better place for everybody.'

This was not the sort of speech which the children had expected, but this was their hero. They listened to what he had to say.

'This is how we could become friends,' Themba continued.

'Over there is the dump. It is the ground that separates us from the people in the New Block. If we, together with them, can build a football field there, then we can stop fighting each other, and start playing football. That is what I want to do. But I shall need help. I don't need money. I need lots of men, women and children to help me. Do you want a football field here in Lapula?'

'YES!!!!' shouted the children.

'Will you help me?'

'YES!!!!' they shouted again.

'Then spread the news around the town. Go home and tell your fathers and mothers, your big brothers and sisters. Tell them I shall call a meeting to talk about this next week. Will you do that?'

'Yes!!!!'

'Thank you, headmaster,' Themba said. 'And thank you, children, for listening to me.'

The headmaster led Themba back to his office. 'That was a very interesting idea, Mr Mtuze,' he said. 'How are you going to get this field built?'

'I shall need your help, headmaster. I would like to form a committee of some of the leading people of the town – like you and Reverend Setuki and others. Then we should call a general meeting. Please could you help me with this? We could invite the parents of some of the children and other people from Old Block and New Block. Could we meet here, in one of your classrooms, one Saturday afternoon?'

The headmaster agreed to hold the meeting in the school. He said he would start by sending messages to the parents, through the children. The teachers would write a notice on the blackboard in each classroom. Then the children would copy this down on a piece of paper and take it home to their parents.

When Themba said goodbye and climbed on to his bicycle, he felt he had made a good start for SHINSA. He set off for the SHINSA flat in Germiston – six kilometres away.

———— ♥ ————

Nomalanga had slept heavily the night before. She woke to find her mother sitting anxiously on her bed shaking her.

'You must get dressed and come to your father at once,' she said. 'Dada wants to speak to you before he goes to the shop.'

Nomalanga dressed quickly and went downstairs. Her father was in the lounge.

'Good morning, Nomalanga,' he said, frowning. 'I hope you slept well. I did not. I lay awake for a long time in the night, thinking about you. Tell me, have I been a bad father? Have I refused to give you food and clothes? Did I beat you when you were a child? What have I done that has made you so angry with me?'

'What do you mean, Dada?' Nomalanga asked. 'I am not angry with you. I love you Dada.'

'You say you love me. Huh! Yet you want to marry that Themba Mtuze,' Mr Ndlovu said. His hands were trembling, he was so angry. There was spit in the corner of his mouth. 'That man is just a common worker.' Nomalanga took in a deep breath to answer him but he held up his hand. 'I say he is a common worker. He works for a builder. He knows nothing. That is bad enough. We also know that he is one of the Old Block gang. He is an enemy of your brother.'

Suddenly Mr Ndlovu's face and voice softened. He reached out for Nomalanga's hand and drew her towards him. 'My child,' he said gently. 'I do love you, and I think you do not know this. That man is a Xhosa.'

'Yes, Dada, I do know that,' Nomalanga said.

Mr Ndlovu frowned. 'Then if you know that, why do you want to marry him? You know that we are Zulus. We do not marry Xhosas.'

'Dada, that is an old idea. People do not think like that now. This is the new South Africa. Themba and I think . . .'

'STOP!' shouted Mr Ndlovu. 'Don't tell me all this rubbish about the new South Africa,' he said. 'I don't want to know about that. And I don't want to know what you and Themba Mtuze think. You will sit down now, and write to Mr Mtuze. You will tell him that it is all finished between the two of you. He must forget about marrying you. Do you hear me?'

'I hear you, Dada,' Nomalanga answered. 'But I cannot.'

'I don't want to hear any arguments,' her father said. 'Either you write that letter, or you get out of this house and never come back.'

'No, you cannot do that,' Mrs Ndlovu said.

'Dudu,' Mr Ndlovu said, turning to his wife. 'Do not tell me what I can and cannot do. I am the father. I say what will happen here in my house. Nomalanga will do what I say. Otherwise, she goes. Do you understand, Nomalanga?'

Nomalanga was silent for a moment. Then she spoke very softly. 'Yes, Dada,' she said. 'I shall go.' She walked out of the room.

Mrs Ndlovu was weeping when she came to Nomalanga's bedroom. 'My child, my child,' she said. 'Go and tell your father you are sorry.'

Nomalanga was busy, packing her suitcase. 'I am not sorry, Mama,' she said. 'I love Dada, but I cannot let him rule my life. I must choose my own path. I will go and stay with Aunt Nonzwakazi. Perhaps Dada will change his mind. I wish he could meet Themba. He is a fine man.'

She put her suitcase once more on the back seat of the Volkswagen and drove to the SHINSA flat.

Aunt Nonzwakazi was just leaving the flat for the office. She saw Nomalanga and wrapped her arms around her as she reached the top of the stairs.

'My little one!' she said. 'Your father has quarrelled with you, hasn't he?' Nomalanga nodded and burst into tears. She put her head on Aunt Nonzwakazi's broad shoulder and the tears just flowed.

'How did you know?' Nomalanga asked.

'This morning I linked through to you,' Aunt Nonzwakazi said. 'I knew you were in trouble. Has your father closed his door on you? I thought so. Come! Sit down, I will make some coffee and we will talk. Your father is a man of the old South Africa,' she said. 'It will take him time to learn new ways. Learning takes time and much pain – especially when you are old. But he will change. You will see.'

While they were talking, they heard the door bell ring. Aunt Nonzwakazi went downstairs to open the door. There was a letter lying on the floor by the front door. She picked it up, and opened the door. Themba was waiting outside. Nomalanga ran downstairs and threw her arms around him. Nomalanga wept on Themba's shoulder, as she told him what her father had said. Her face was swollen, and her eyes were red from crying.

At last they went upstairs and sat on the chairs in the middle of the room. He held her hand, trying to comfort her.

Aunt Nonzwakazi sat at one of the desks, and opened the letter she had found in the passage. It was a fat letter which had come from England. Presently, Nomalanga got up to make coffee for Themba. She seemed calmer.

'Aunt Nonzwakazi says it will take time for my Dada to learn new ways,' Nomalanga said. 'But I don't think I can work for him any more in the council. He will not want me to be his secretary. I will have to find another job.'

Aunt Nonzwakazi smiled. 'It is a wonderful thing in life,' she said. 'Whenever one door closes, another door opens. You want another job, Nomalanga?' She held up the letter in her hand. 'The job has come this minute in the post. Look at this.' She peeled away a thick bundle of papers. 'These are the names and addresses of all the people Mr Evans met when he was touring round South Africa. Remember, he is the "Technical Aid" man from England. He wants me to be his agent here in South Africa. I must write to all these people, find out what they plan to do and what they need. Then I send the information to him. If I agree, then he will send me a cheque to buy a computer and employ a secretary. How would you like to be the SHINSA secretary, Nomalanga?'

Nomalanga stood up and threw her arms around Aunt Nonzwakazi. 'Happy day! Happy day!' she cried. Then she ran across to Themba and threw her arms around him. Then she pulled him across so that she could put one arm around each of them. She started dancing and singing, 'Joy! Joy! Joy!' It was a hymn that they sang in church. Themba knew the hymn and joined in, singing the bass part in his deep voice. All this was too much for Aunt Nonzwakazi. She started panting and was allowed to go and sit down, while Nomalanga went across and made the usual cup of coffee.

Then they settled down to think and plan carefully how they were going to organise the affairs of Aunt Nonzwakazi's SHINSA, and Themba's football field project. It was agreed that Nomalanga would be secretary for both her aunt and Themba, but first she would have to learn how to work on a computer.

Time for Work!

Themba stood on the back of the lorry and looked out over the dump. It was amazing. Everywhere he looked, he could see groups of men and women, teenage boys and girls all working away in the warm sunlight.

Each group had one man as a leader to direct them. In some groups, the men were cutting down the trees and bushes with big axes and saws. The boys and girls then dragged these to another place, where the women cut the branches into small pieces for firewood. These were then made into bundles and loaded on donkey-carts and taken to the secondary school for sale. Other groups were already busy with the levelling. The ground sloped slightly down towards the dry river-bed. So the task was to dig the ground away on one side, and move it to the other. Themba had set pegs in the ground to mark the places where the earth had to be dug out, and other ones where it was to be banked up. It was quite amazing how enthusiastic the people were about the Lapula football field.

The first meeting Themba held, however, had been a disappointment. He had invited Reverend Setuki and some of the members of the town council to meet in the secondary school. He had told them about the scheme and asked for their opinion. They had said that they did not think the people would want to do the work. It would cost a lot of money and take too long. It would be better to try to raise the money by selling secondhand clothes, or sending boys and girls to clean other people's motor cars. With this money, they could then hire bulldozers. When the wise old men had gone, Themba sat at the school desk and put his head down in his hands. It was hopeless, he thought. Nobody could get excited about selling old clothes. And if they hired bulldozers, his own skills as an engineer would never be used.

'Worry! Worry! Worry!' said the headmaster cheerfully. 'Worry will get you nowhere, my friend. You had a dream, that day you came to talk to my children. You shared that dream with us. We also saw the beautiful green football field shining in the sunlight. Now, you must make that dream come true. Forget about those old men. They are too old to have dreams. They only have memories.'

So Themba went ahead. With the help of Nomalanga, he put up the posters calling for a general meeting. The children took the notices to their parents and, on the Sunday morning of the meeting, the people came in their hundreds. Aunt Nonzwakazi had given him the money to hire some scaffolding to make a platform, and to hire a loud-speaker system on a van. The Cats had agreed to come and play a few of their numbers. Themba and Nomalanga also sang their famous song, 'Hullo there, Sunshine!' People clapped and clapped. They had to sing it twice.

Then Themba had made his speech. First, he had talked about how foolish it was to have a gang war between the New Block and the Old Block. Then he had talked about the dump and how it could be made into a football field, so that people from both parts of Lapula could play football, instead of fighting. Lastly, he had talked about how this could be done by the people themselves. Then he called for names and addresses of those who were willing to work, or to lend tools, or to help raise money.

The response was overwhelming. Six hundred and forty-three people put their names down on to lists. Some of them wanted to start work immediately but Aunt Nonzwakazi advised Themba not to be in a hurry.

'Yoh! We must organise this properly, my boy,' she said. 'You don't know people. Today they will kiss you, tomorrow they will have forgotten your name. We must work through the lists, choose people from the same areas to work together. Then they can chase each other to work. You will need new tyres for your bicycle by the time you have finished organising them into groups.'

She was right. It took time, and before they got started, many people changed their minds. But this was now the third Sunday of working, and most of the bush was cleared and the land was very nearly level. There was still work to be done in building up the bank. The sand from the river-bed was quite good sand, and they had collected enough money to buy cement. So Themba hoped to make a wall to hold the bank and drain the water. Then, one day, they would put a fence around it, build changing-rooms, and put some wooden benches on the bank.

'Hey you!' said a voice. 'Are you the big man in charge – Themba Mtuze?' A very fat man leaned out of the window of a very old Buick.

'Yes, I am,' Themba replied. 'What do you want?'

The man climbed heavily out of the car. 'I am Mahlelebe,' the man said. 'I am a reporter for *The Soweto News*. You have probably heard of me. No? Well, it doesn't matter then. Your girl-friend here told me about your scheme.'

Themba looked into the car and was surprised to see Nomalanga sitting in the passenger's seat. She was laughing as she came and put her arms around Themba's neck and gave him a kiss on the cheek.

'He wouldn't wait, Themba,' she said. 'I phoned him this morning, to ask if he was interested in your scheme for making a football field. I told him a bit about it. Half an hour later he was hooting outside Aunt Nonzwakazi's flat. He said he wanted to see you straightaway.'

'That's right. She's smart, this girl of yours,' Mr Mahlelebe said. 'She knows that publicity is better than a bulldozer. It works faster. One article from the great Mahlelebe and you will have enough money to finish this job. OK?' He turned round to shout to a tall, thin man who was sitting in the back of the Buick. 'Hey! Johnny. Come and shoot this man immediately.'

Themba got a shock, until he saw that the tall, thin man was carrying a camera, not a gun. Johnny took a number of photographs, happy pictures of happy people. Meanwhile, Mr Mahlelebe talked to Themba.

For the next few days, Themba paid regular visits to the Ramona Cafe, next door to Aunt Nonzwakazi's flat to look at copies of *The Soweto News*, but there was nothing in there about his project.

Then on the Saturday morning after Mr Mahlelebe's visit, when Themba arrived on his bicycle, Mr Papolous, the owner of the cafe, was waiting outside his shop on the veranda.

'Hey you big man!' he shouted. 'It has come. You better come look-see.' He led the way into his shop, and there on the counter he had laid out *The Soweto News*, open at the page. There were three pictures, one of Nomalanga and Themba, with a faraway dreamy look in their eyes, and a few figures of children dragging thorn-bushes in the background. The other two pictures were of the workers, all looking very pleased with themselves.

Below this were three columns of print, which told the story. Of course, Mr Mahlelebe had made some mistakes. He said that Themba was a qualified engineer from Fort Hare. He said that Nomalanga was the daughter of Mrs Nonzwakazi. He said that the Lapula Secondary School had two thousand pupils – instead of two hundred. But the main part of the story – about SHINSA and the plan to build a football field in the dump – was all correct. 'All this is being done by the people themselves, without any help from anyone outside,' the article said. 'We cannot help wondering why the Lapula Town Council have not offered to help in some way – even a bag of cement would be something.'

Themba bought four copies of the paper and took it

straight up into the flat to show the others. Aunt Nonzwakazi sat in one of the armchairs and read one copy. Nomalanga and Themba put another copy on the dining-room table and stood, side by side with their arms around each other's waists, reading it. Aunt Nonzwakazi finished first. She did not have to stop now and again to kiss anybody as Themba and Nomalanga were doing.

'Hah!' she said. 'Now you are famous. This will make a big difference. You will see. Any minute from now, the phone will ring. And I'll tell you another thing. Your father, Nomalanga, will forget about the war between Zulus and Xhosas.'

She was right, of course. Within an hour, Mrs Ndlovu phoned up to say she had been thinking of coming to see Aunt Nonzwakazi. Would that afternoon be convenient? A bit later, the secretary of the Soweto Men's Club phoned to say that the club had some old fence posts and wire which they would like to give to the SHINSA project. A seed merchant in Germiston offered a sack of grass-seed, and another man offered some plastic piping, so that they could pump water to the field. It was all happening so fast, it felt as though they were in a bus running down hill at top speed.

That afternoon, the big black Mercedes pulled up outside Ramona Cafe. Not only Mrs Ndlovu got out, but also Cuthbert and Mr Ndlovu himself. Nomalanga threw her arms around her mother's neck, and there were tears in her eyes. Then she put her arms around her father's neck and then Cuthbert's. Mr Ndlovu found it difficult to shake hands with Themba. He stood there, stiff and straight and held out his hand for Themba to shake. But he managed to do it, and he even managed a small smile.

'I hope we can forget the quarrels of the past,' he said very solemnly. 'I made a mistake about you, my boy, I see that you are a good man. Nomalanga said you were, and she was right. I would like us to be friends now.'

Themba thanked Mr Ndlovu. 'I think you know, sir,' he said respectfully, 'that I love Nomalanga, and I want to marry her.'

Mr Ndlovu bowed and said Nomalanga had told him that. 'Since reading the article in the newspaper about the work you are doing at the dump,' he said, 'I have spoken to some of my friends in the council. We have agreed that we can give you enough money to employ ten labourers for a month. Will that help you to finish off the job?'

Themba said that he thought it would. So Mr Ndlovu promised to come and see the work in a few days' time. In the meantime, Themba was to go ahead and employ ten men.

14

Disaster Strikes

During the following weeks the new arrangement with Mr Ndlovu and the council worked well. Themba had no difficulty in finding ten good men to help him. They soon finished levelling the field, then the grass-seed was sown and watered and small green shoots began to appear. Meanwhile, the men had erected the fence posts around the field, and strung out the wires.

Every Friday morning, Themba would receive a pay-sheet and cheque in the post. He would cash the cheque at the post office, and that afternoon he would pay the men. The job was coming to an end now. They only had to make the bank into terraces, and make seats from some second-hand wooden planks they had bought. Then the job would be finished.

Themba was so busy that he spent less and less time at the Ngxolos'. Noluvuyo would often visit him at the dump while he was working. She missed not seeing him so much at home. Themba did not have much time for chatting but he would ask after the family and exchange the odd joke with her.

Nomalanga spent most of her time at the SHINSA flat working on her aunt's and Themba's projects for SHINSA. Sometimes, when she had time, she would slip out and go down to the dump to watch Themba at work. She marvelled at his ability to organise the men, and encourage them to work quickly and efficiently. However, she often noticed Noluvuyo there talking and laughing with Themba. Nomalanga was not jealous, but something kept worrying her when she saw them together.

One evening, Aunt Nonzwakazi suddenly made a surprising announcement. 'Tomorrow, I must leave you two little doves,' she said to Themba and Nomalanga, 'and go back to my wagon-puppies.'

'Why? What's gone wrong?' Nomalanga asked.

'I have to go and talk to the Child Welfare Committee. I'll be away about a week. Do you think you two can manage for a week without me?'

'We shall miss you,' Themba said. 'But we shall manage.' He had come to love Aunt Nonzwakazi, as if she were his own mother. He loved her for her strength and her cheerfulness. She never seemed to be unhappy. Nothing ever made her give up hope. And with people, she either liked them, or hated them. She always told everyone exactly what she thought. You always knew where you were with Aunt Nonzwakazi.

The evening after the aunt's departure, Nomalanga and Themba were alone together in the SHINSA flat. Themba wanted Nomalanga to sit on his lap in the big chair, but Nomalanga refused. She made excuses that she was feeling too hot and tired. Themba went up to her and put his arm about her and asked, 'What's wrong, dear one? Don't you love me any more?'

Nomalanga pushed him away and answered, 'I don't know.' She looked away, and a tear rolled down her cheek.

Themba began to feel very worried. His face was full of concern as he said, 'Nomalanga, Nomalanga, my love. We must be truthful to one another. Please tell me what's bothering you.'

'Well,' Nomalanga began, 'how do I know what you do, or where you go when you are not with me?'

Themba laughed. 'Do you think I have other girl-friends?' he asked and tried to tickle her, but she pushed him away again. Themba felt anger growing inside him like a sickness. 'So you think I deceive you?' he said. 'You think I have lots of girl-friends? If that is what you think, then we had better say goodbye now.'

Nomalanga clutched his hand and drew him back. 'No, it's not that, Themba. It's that . . . Aunt Nonzwakazi gave me something to read recently. It was an article about AIDS. It said that thousands of people in South Africa had AIDS. Sometimes I've seen you with Noluvuyo, laughing and talking. It made me think that I don't know what girl-friends you have had before you met me. How do I know if you have got AIDS or not? That's what worries me.' She put her face in her hands and wept.

Themba put his arm comfortingly around her shoulder. 'Don't cry, my dear one,' he said. 'If that is what is worrying you, then I shall go tomorrow to the hospital. They can test me for AIDS. I am quite sure I haven't got it, but let them prove it to you. Will you be happy then?'

'Oh, Themba, will you do this for me?' Nomalanga said. She stood up and threw herself into his arms. 'I know it is silly, but I have been so worried since I read that article. Dear Themba, thank you for being so understanding. Can you go tomorrow?'

They agreed on this. The next morning Themba rode off to Luthuli Hospital and went to the out-patients clinic. He sat for an hour in the waiting-room, with children crying and old men coughing and spitting around him. At last he was called into the surgery. He asked the doctor to test him for AIDS. He had to fill in some forms and then the doctor did the tests. Themba was told that he would receive the results by post.

Themba came out of the clinic and was walking down the long corridor to the exit, when he heard somebody behind him shouting.

'Hey! You, Themba! Do you no longer know the people who cared for you?' said the voice. Themba turned round and found it was Sister Mathebula. She seemed really pleased to see him. She had read the article in *The Soweto News* about the football field, she said, and she had seen the picture of him with Nomalanga.

'How is your girl-friend?' Sister Mathebula asked. 'When is the baby due?'

'Baby! What baby?' Themba asked in amazement.

'Oh, are you also going to pretend there is no baby?' Sister Mathebula said, laughing. 'Your girl-friend said the same when she came to visit you. But I know about these things. If she is not pregnant, why did she faint in my office?'

'Did she faint in your office?' Themba asked. 'Does that mean she is pregnant?'

Sister Mathebula nodded and said, 'When a young girl faints in the morning, it usually means she is pregnant.'

'Well, she does not faint now,' Themba said.

'No, of course not,' Sister Mathebula replied. 'That only happens in the first few weeks. So you are going to be a Dada, hey Themba? Anyway, it has been nice seeing you again. Goodbye!' She waved cheerily and went off down the corridor, leaving Themba to fight with some very cruel thoughts.

'Is Nomalanga pregnant?' Themba thought. 'If she is pregnant, then who is the father? I have not made love to her. I suppose the father has refused to marry her. So now she wants me to marry her. But . . . but . . . I still love her.' He could see her now in his mind's eye, smiling at him with that special smile that made her eyes light up. He felt an aching pain in his chest. What was he to do?

As soon as Themba got off his bicycle in the back yard, Mrs Ngxolo knew that something was wrong. Instead of smiling and greeting her, he threw his bike against the wall and started walking off to his room.

'I have made some tea,' she called out to him. 'Would you like some?'

He came across and accepted a cup, and in five minutes

he had told her all about his problem. He could not help himself. Mrs Ngxolo was a motherly person – very easy to talk to. She was also in no doubt as to what was the best thing to do.

'You must write and tell her that it is all finished between you,' Mrs Ngxolo said. 'You will never be able to trust that woman again, Themba. If she has started deceiving you now, she will go on all through your married life. It is no good. And the child too, when it grows up, will be like the mother. You will just have one long life of unhappiness. No, Themba, no. I am so sorry for you. But my advice is, go now, before it is too late. Do not go and see her. She is too pretty. She will make you weak. Write a letter to her, and then go away from Lapula. Go and find a job in East London or Cape Town or somewhere else far away.'

Themba nodded slowly. What Mrs Ngxolo said was sensible and true. 'Thank you, Mama,' he said. 'Thank you for the tea and the advice.'

Then he went to his room, took out his writing pad and wrote two letters. The first was to Mr Ndlovu. He told him that he had decided to resign from the job at the football field. He suggested that one of the new employees should be put in charge.

The second letter was the hardest letter he had ever had to write. It was to Nomalanga. First he wrote accusing her of deceiving him. It became a long, childish letter. He tore it up and started again, and tore up two more letters. At last he wrote just these few words.

Dear Nomalanga,
This morning I met Sister Mathebula at the hospital. I think you know what she told me. I have decided to leave Lapula and go and work somewhere else. I am sorry that you were not able to tell me the truth. Please give my best wishes to Aunt Nonzwakazi. Tell her, I hope that SHINSA is a great success.

I have written to your father and asked him to find someone else to finish the job at the football field.

I hope the baby is beautiful. I would have been happy to be the father, if only you had told me about it. I will always love you. Yours, Themba.

He went out and posted both of these letters. Then he thought he would go to the beer hall and get drunk. But when he saw how stupid the other drunk men were, he got back on to his bicycle and rode home. He quietly got into bed, read for a while and went to sleep.

That night, he dreamt about Nomalanga. He dreamt that she came to him, carrying a baby in her arms. 'There's your Dada, my baby,' she said and put the baby on to his lap. The baby looked like Mr Gumede. Themba woke up sweating.

──────── ♥ ────────

While Nomalanga was waiting for Themba to come back, she prepared a special supper for him. He would soon be with her. Then she could hug him and kiss him and tell him she loved him. They would sit down together and eat the big pieces of steak she had cooked. They would eat the watermelon which she had bought from Mr Papolous. They would sit together on the couch and kiss.

But Themba did not come. The food got cold. At first she was angry. Then she was worried. Finally she became afraid. Something must have happened to him. He must have been knocked down in an accident. Perhaps she should phone the police – or the hospital. She went to bed but could not sleep for a long, long time.

She woke up the next morning to hear the phone ringing in the office. She went through, lifted the receiver and heard her father's voice.

'Hullo, is that you, Nomalanga? What's happened to Themba?'

'I don't know. Why do you ask?'

'A letter has just come from him in the post,' Mr Ndlovu said. 'He has resigned his job. He does not say why. He says you will explain. What's happening?'

Nomalanga felt as though the floor had fallen away and she was dropping to the ground. She did not know what to say. She stood, holding the phone, and time passed without her knowledge.

'Hullo!. . . Hullo Nomalanga!. . . Are you there?. . . Nomalanga, can you hear me?' Her father's voice kept asking but she did not hear him. She could not answer. At last she put the phone down without saying anything. She stood for a moment gazing at the wall. Then she knew that there must be a letter waiting for her in the passage, at the bottom of the stairs, by the front door.

She ran down the stairs and there was Themba's letter. She leant against the big, wooden cupboard and ripped it open, and as she read the words he had written, it was as though a knife cut across her chest. She burst out crying and ran upstairs, straight back to the bedroom. She threw herself on the bed and started weeping. She wept and wept until no more tears would come. Then she stood up and dressed herself. But every time she saw the letter lying on the bed, she started to weep again.

———♥———

Mr Papolous, the owner of the Ramona Cafe, had also had a rough night. His wife had gone to Greece on a holiday, to see her father and mother. She had not seen them since she and Mr Papolous left Greece in 1961. She was supposed to stay for a month and then fly back again. Instead, she had written to say that she was not coming back. She wanted to stay with her father and mother and help run the olive farm. So, he could either sell the shop and come and join her, she wrote, or he could stay on his own in the Ramona Cafe. She was never coming back.

Mr Papolous pulled the bedclothes away from his face. The sun was shining in his eyes. He had drunk a bottle of brandy the night before. He felt sick. He knew there was only one thing that would make him feel better – another bottle of brandy. There was a whole case in a cupboard under the stairs, behind the spare gas cylinders. He kept a small gas stove to use when the electricity was not working.

He got out of bed, opened the cupboard door and lifted out one of the gas cylinders. He put it carefully on top of the electric stove – out of the way. Then he got out a bottle of brandy and poured himself a good measure. Ah!!! That felt better. He felt the burning spirit go down into his fat stomach and warm his body and mind. Any minute now, he thought, the people would start hammering on the door of the shop. It was late. But first, he must have some food. He would fry some bacon and sausages and make some coffee. He switched on the electric stove and went back to the bedroom to dress himself. He did not notice that he had switched on the wrong electric hotplate. The one that was burning was the one under the gas cylinder.

———— ♥ ————

Mr Ndlovu was worried when he heard the line go dead. 'Dudu!' he said, as he put the phone down. 'Our girl is in trouble. That Xhosa has disappeared. I knew there was something wrong there. We must go and help the child. Get dressed. Get some food. We must go there immediately.'

While Mrs Ndlovu was dressing, Mr Ndlovu told Cuthbert to go to Boxers and open the shop for him. Cuthbert was to tell the assistant manager that his father would come to the shop at eleven o'clock. A few minutes later, Mr and Mrs Ndlovu were both in the car, speeding towards the SHINSA flat in Germiston.

Nomalanga's eyes were red and her face was swollen from crying when she opened the door to let them in. But she was able to talk sensibly about what had happened. She said that she would like her father to take her to Twenty-three Street to see Themba. She showed them into the flat and then went across to the office to get her jersey.

———— ♥ ————

Meanwhile Themba was preparing to leave. He packed his clothes into a suitcase, and his tools into a wooden box. Mrs Ngxolo came to see how he was getting on, and handed him a letter which had arrived that morning. It contained the results of the AIDS test: Themba had not got AIDS. He thought miserably how pleased Nomalanga would have been with the news, and how happy they would have been. But now he was never going to see her again.

As he was about to leave he remembered his books. He had taken them to Aunt Nonzwakazi's flat, to discuss various building projects for SHINSA with her. These books contained all sorts of valuable information and he did not want to leave without them. He decided he would have to go to the flat to pick them up.

He had his own key to the flat. Perhaps Nomalanga would have gone home, he thought. Or if she were in the flat, he would creep into the office and get his books without anybody knowing. But what if she saw him? He was afraid of seeing her again. He knew that, if he just saw her, those feelings of love and desire would come over him. He would want to take her in his arms and comfort her. He would forget about the baby. But, no, he must be brave and sensible. He must go there and get his books back. And if he saw her, he would just say coldly, 'I have come for my books.' There was nothing she could do to make him change his mind.

He took the well-known road to Germiston and arrived outside the Ramona Cafe. As he put his bicycle against the veranda wall, the whole building exploded in front of his eyes. It threw him to the ground and the bicycle on top of him. The door was blown from its hinges and smashed into a car parked in front of it. There was the sound of breaking glass and immediately he could see flames coming from the Ramona Cafe and Sammy's Supermarket.

Themba stood up and looked at the SHINSA flat above him. The windows had been blown out and the roof had collapsed on top of the rooms. Without thinking of any danger to himself, he ran in through the open door.

He could smell burning and already there was thick smoke in the passage. The stairs were smashed to pieces. There seemed to be no way of getting up them. By some miracle, the big cupboard was not broken. It took all his strength to drag it across to where the stairs had been. He was then able to climb on to the cupboard. He could now hear cries coming from the flat and this made him desperate. He reached up to an overhanging beam and pulled himself on to what was left of the landing.

The door to the flat had collapsed. The top of the door frame was holding up part of the wall. He managed to push the frame up and crawl underneath. Inside the living-room Mrs Ndlovu was lying moaning on the floor, with Mr Ndlovu bending over her, shaking her. 'Dudu, my darling. Dudu! Dudu!' he kept saying.

Themba climbed over the up-turned dining-table to the kitchen sink. Water was squirting out of a broken pipe. He caught some in a cup and took it to Mr Ndlovu. Mr Ndlovu looked at it blankly. So Themba poured some of the water on to Mrs Ndlovu's face. She moved and then opened her eyes. He gave her the rest of the water to drink. Then she sat up.

'What happened?' she asked.

'You must get out of here,' Themba said. 'The building is on fire. Where is Nomalanga?'

Mr Ndlovu seemed able to think again, now that his wife

was better. He helped her to her feet. Then he said to Themba, 'Nomalanga went through to the office.'

Themba nodded. He pointed to the hole where the doorway to the flat had been. 'You will have to crawl through there,' he explained. Again, he forced his way through, then he held up the wall, by lifting the top of the door frame. Mr and Mrs Ndlovu crawled through. The three of them were now standing on a concrete shelf, which used to be the landing. There were dense clouds of smoke coming up from the passage.

'You must go down on to that cupboard,' Themba shouted, pointing downwards.

Mr Ndlovu nodded. 'I'll go first,' he said. He knelt down, gripped the edge of the shelf and then lowered himself on to the top of the cupboard. He put up his hands to help Mrs Ndlovu, but she stood looking in fear at the flames and the smoke below. She was too afraid to move.

Themba picked her up around the waist and lowered her down to the waiting arms of her husband.

'You are all right, my darling,' Mr Ndlovu said as he caught her.

There was a sudden crack and the cupboard split apart, tipping Mr and Mrs Ndlovu on to the ground. They rolled over, but both got up again. The wood of the cupboard was now burning fiercely, which was why it had broken. Themba saw Mr and Mrs Ndlovu staggering away through the smoke and flames to the entrance. They were safe. Now he must find Nomalanga. Themba found that the office door had jammed when the roof fell on it. It was not possible to open it. But somewhere inside the office, Nomalanga was trapped. He must get to her. Flames from the burning cupboard started to lick the walls. The smoke made him cough. He took a handkerchief from his pocket and held it over his mouth and nose. Now he could breathe through the handkerchief. The office door was a strong, solid wooden door.

He picked up one of the big slabs of concrete from the broken landing, and smashed a hole in the door. Then he climbed through the hole and started looking for Nomalanga. There was not yet much smoke in the office.

Nomalanga was standing in the corner, where the window had been crushed down by the roof. She was crying with terror, and trying to pull the bricks from the broken wall. She turned round when he shouted at her, but she did not recognise him. He took away the handkerchief from his face. Then a look of wonder came into her eyes. 'You have come?' she said. Themba held out his arms and she ran across, weeping with joy. He kissed the tears on her cheeks and eyelashes.

Smoke was now coming in through the hole in the door. Themba could see the flames from the burning cupboard on the other side. 'We cannot get out that way,' he said. There was a coat hanging on a hook, on the back of the door. He took it down and stuffed it into the hole. The smoke stopped, but he knew that the flames would soon burn the door down. They must get out before that happened.

He went across to where the window used to be. There was now no window. The weight of the roof had crushed the window frame. The wall was crumbling. Soon the roof would fall on top of them. He put his shoulder under one of the roof beams and lifted it. This made a small hole. It was big enough for Nomalanga to crawl through. Then she could jump down to the ground.

'Quick, Nomalanga!' he grunted. 'Get out!'

Before she could do so, another part of the roof shifted. More of the wall fell away. The hole was closed. Themba was forced on to his knees. He lowered the beam and stood up. Smoke started coming in through the broken roof. They could hear the flames roaring and crackling in the flat. Soon the office would be on fire too. Nomalanga started to cough from the smoke.

'There is no way out now, Nomalanga,' Themba said. 'We will die here.'

Nomalanga did not seem to be afraid. She took Themba's hand, and led him across to the corner by the hand-basin. There was less smoke here. 'My dear one,' she said. She looked up into his face. 'I don't mind dying, as long as I know that you love me.'

Themba put his arms around her. 'I am sorry, my love. I'm sorry that I wrote that letter,' he said. 'I love you. Why did you not tell me about the baby?'

'What baby?' Nomalanga asked, frowning. 'I have no baby.'

Themba was confused. 'I saw Sister Mathebula at the hospital. She said . . .'

'What did she say?' Nomalanga asked. Suddenly she remembered that morning in the hospital – when she had fainted. 'I'm not pregnant,' she said. 'I fainted in the hospital, because Sister Mathebula told me you were dying.'

Themba looked down. Their eyes met. His arms went around her, and she buried her face in his shoulder. 'It's the truth, my dear Themba,' she said. 'I love you.' They started to kiss. Suddenly, in the middle of the kiss, Nomalanga stopped and drew away from him. 'Look, Themba!' She pointed to the wall. There, hanging above the sink, was the large fire extinguisher. They had both seen it many times, and they had both forgotten about it.

'Quick!' said Themba. 'Make those towels wet.' He took down two towels from the rack and handed them to her. There was water in a plastic basin in the sink. She soaked both the towels in the water. Meanwhile he lifted down the extinguisher from the wall and carried it across to the doorway and put it down.

'There are flames out there,' he shouted, pointing to the door. 'And lots of smoke. You must cover your face with the towel. I'll go first and put out the fire. When I shout, you must come.' They could hear the flames roaring loudly.

Themba pulled the coat out of the hole. Immediately, a cloud of smoke and one orange tongue of flame came through the hole. Themba covered his face and crawled through. Nomalanga saw his legs disappear. Then there was a hissing sound and clouds of white smoke. The flames seemed to disappear. Themba shouted, 'COME! COME!' She covered her nose and mouth with the wet towel and crawled through the hole. She found herself on the broken landing. Below her, where there used to be stairs, there was now nothing. Themba was standing below her, on a heap of smoking ashes. He was holding out his arms ready to catch her. She jumped, and felt his hands go under her armpits, hold her, and then lower her to the ground.

They stumbled out into the open. There was a crowd of people standing in the car-park, watching. They gave a cheer when they saw Themba and Nomalanga come out of the burning building. Amongst them were Mr and Mrs Ndlovu. They were standing beside the Mercedes. Mr Ndlovu came across to help Nomalanga.

'What has happened to Mr Papolous?' Themba asked.

Mr Ndlovu shrugged his shoulders and pointed to the ruined cafe. 'I think he must be dead!' he said gravely.

15

A New Day Dawns

The blue dress certainly suited Mrs Ndlovu. 'I think the person who made this dress, made it specially for me,' she said to Cuthbert, who was driving her in the black Mercedes to the church for the wedding of Nomalanga and Themba. She was to go to the church first, to welcome all the people. Mr Ndlovu and Nomalanga were to follow later, in a taxi.

When they arrived at the church there already seemed to be a lot of people gathering. Mrs Ndlovu recognised some from New Block. There must have also been some from Old Block, she thought, because she did not recognise them. She was a little angry to see Reverend Setuki standing at the door of the church, waiting to welcome people. 'After all,' she thought, 'it is our wedding. I should be there to welcome the people.' She got out of the car and greeted those she knew. Then she went and stood beside him. Some of the congregation inside started singing hymns as usual.

'Where is the bridegroom?' Reverend Setuki asked. 'He has not arrived yet.'

'I hope he is coming,' Mrs Ndlovu said. She saw Mr Gumede standing by the church door. 'Perhaps Themba has run away again, Mr Gumede,' she called out. 'If he has, then you can marry Nomalanga.' Mr Gumede's serious eyes shone with excitement.

A taxi drove up to the church. The doors burst open and a man, a woman and seven children, of different ages and sizes, climbed out. They all started talking at once. The eldest girl, a long-legged schoolgirl, came running across to Mrs Ndlovu.

'Your dress . . . it looks beautiful,' she said with shining eyes. She lifted the hem of Mrs Ndlovu's dress and rubbed it between her fingers and thumb. 'It is very good quality,' she said, nodding. 'Our teacher at the secondary school says you must always be sure to get good quality cloth.'

'Thank you, my child,' Mrs Ndlovu said firmly, pushing Noluvuyo's hand away. 'I always get the best.' She greeted Mr and Mrs Ngxolo.

'Themba is just coming,' Mrs Ngxolo said.

'How do you know?' Mrs Ndlovu asked.

'He lives in my house,' Mrs Ngxolo explained. 'He ordered another taxi.'

'Well, I hope he hurries up,' Mrs Ndlovu said. The Ngxolo family joined the congregation in the church.

Next to arrive was a large bus. It pulled up in a cloud of dust and the door burst open. First to get out was a man in a gold and purple robe. It was Bishop Ngcobo. He was followed by the choir in their white and purple robes. Then came Mrs Lenaka and about twenty children. The girls were neatly dressed in little white frocks. The boys wore black short trousers and white shirts. Last of all came Aunt Nonzwakazi. She was not wearing her choir dress. Instead she had bought, specially for the occasion, a bright red and gold material which she had had made into a kaftan. It was wrapped around her large body and gleamed in the sunlight. It made her look like a queen. In her hands she carried her plastic cross and she took her place at the head of the choir.

'One, two, three, four,' Aunt Nonzwakazi shouted. The choir all started singing 'Glory! Glory! Hallelujah!' and they marched towards the church door. Reverend Setuki and Mrs Ndlovu had to step aside to let them pass. Aunt Nonzwakazi's sleeve caught Mrs Ndlovu's hat and knocked it off. But Aunt Nonzwakazi did not seem to notice this. She led the way into the church, and they marched up the aisle. Then Aunt Nonzwakazi turned around and lowered the cross. This was the signal for them to stop singing, so they went and found seats for themselves.

Mrs Ndlovu put her hat back on and smoothed down her beautiful blue dress. Themba had still not arrived. He was supposed to come early and wait for the bride in the church. If he did not come soon, Mr Ndlovu and Nomalanga would get there ahead of him. Some more people arrived and then they heard the sound of a bicycle bell. Themba appeared, pedalling away as hard as he could. The sweat was pouring off him. Makalima was sitting on the crossbar of the bicycle.

'I'm sorry . . . Mrs Ndlovu,' Themba said. He was panting hard. 'The taxi came late,' he said. 'Then it had a puncture.' He gasped for breath. 'I could not wait . . . I came on my bicycle.'

'Who is this?' Mrs Ndlovu asked, pointing with a blue-gloved finger at Makalima.

'He is my best man,' Themba said.

'Is that the best you could find?' she asked. 'All right then. Go in, go in,' she said. 'And stop panting.'

Themba and Makalima went to the front of the church and stood waiting at the altar.

'Themba,' Makalima said softly. 'I think I had better give this to you now. When we get to the party after the service, and start drinking, I will forget about it.' He pulled an envelope out of his pocket and handed it to Themba.

'What is it?' Themba asked.

'It's your wedding present, remember? I promised, if that little harmonica brought you and Nomalanga together, I would pay back the fifty rands.'

'I did not think you were serious,' Themba said. He peeped into the envelope. There, sure enough, was a bundle of five-rand notes inside.

'And I have kept my promise,' Makalima said. 'I have not stolen any more cars. I nearly did, last week. But I stopped myself in time. But I did drive Cuthbert's motor bike!'

'You stole his bike?' Themba asked.

'No,' Makalima laughed. 'He was sitting behind me on

the pillion. We are friends now. I am going to buy his bike from him. He is getting a new one.'

Suddenly, everyone could hear the sound of a car hooting outside. The congregation stopped singing. There was silence for a moment. Then the people sitting by the church door started talking excitedly and pointing. They started singing a hymn which Nomalanga had chosen specially. It was a hymn that said love lasts forever.

Reverend Setuki came down the aisle and stood waiting at the altar. Then Mr Ndlovu appeared at the door, with Nomalanga on his arm. She was dressed all in white, in a silk dress that went down to the ground. She had a veil over her face and was carrying a bunch of red roses. It seemed to Themba, as he saw her walking slowly, with dignity, towards him, that this was surely the most beautiful sight he had ever seen in his whole life. The congregation stopped singing and watched as Themba put out his hand to her. 'Hullo there, Sunshine,' he said. She smiled and placed her hand in his.

Then they joined in the singing. Themba sang in his deep bass voice, Nomalanga sang in her clear soprano voice, their two young voices blending in perfect harmony: 'Eternal love in us abide.'

They turned to face the Reverend – and their whole future in the new South Africa – together.

HEINEMANN HEARTBEATS

The book you have been reading is part of the new Heinemann Heartbeats series. Details of some of the other titles available are listed below.

♥

A Bride for the King
NANDI DLOVU

Beautiful Zible dearly loves Saul. Then the royal *sangoma* declares the Zible will marry Saul's half-brother – the king. The young lovers are heart-broken. Against a background of sorcery and intrigue, Zible prepares to meet her fate . . .

♥

Stolen Kisses
MICHELLE MWANSA

Shy schoolgirl Patience meets young lawyer Artwell Nkosi in the library. She is swept off her feet. Is this true love, or is Artwell really after her sister, the glamorous model Thandiwe?

♥

The Gift of Life
PATRICIA CAGE

When Thembi wins the heart of Mduduzi, everyone agrees that this is a match made in heaven. Suddenly, at their engagement party, disaster strikes. Will things ever be the same again?

♥

Please Forgive Me
ROSINA UMELO

Oke and Bukky love each other dearly. But Oke's sister, Udoka, will have nothing to do with the girlfriend she calls a witch. Oke and Udoka are involved in a tragic car accident and suddenly it all looks like Bukky's fault . . .

Heart of Love
HOPE DUBE

Claudette is hard-working and new to the company. She is bright and beautiful. Charles Daka is her boss, and is rich, successful and single. How can Claudette get him to take her seriously and find her attractive?

Love Changes Everything
KALU OKPI

In exile in Nigeria, stylish Gavinah finds love in the arms of Onyeukwu, law student and rock musician. But her tragic past soon catches up with her and it seems that the young lovers will never be together . . .

The Jasmine Candle
CHRISTINE A. BOTCHWAY

Zenobia, a mysterious beauty, lives a lonely life in a land between two ancient tribes. Even her childhood friend Odole doesn't want to know her. Then she breaks a taboo and Odole is ordered to kill her. Our heroine seems doomed.

Love Snare
JAMES IRUNGU

Sweet, innocent Emma is excited when she lands an important new job. She hasn't bargained for her new manager – the ruthless playboy J. N. Mwea. Mwea's old flame wants to capture him again. Emma's very life is soon in danger

---

The Place of Gentle Waters
JESSICA MAJI

Scientist Anne Caldwell arrives from Britain to go to Richard Giba's Kenyan farm to help him with a problem. She soon finds herself attracted to him. But Anne had a dark secret . . .